SECOND SKIN

SECOND SKIN

Jessica Wollman

Delacorte Press

Copyright © 2009 by Jessica Wollman

Delacorte Press is a registered trademark and the colophon is a trademark of Random House, Inc.

Visit us on the Web! www.randomhouse.com/teens

Educators and librarians, for a variety of teaching tools, visit us at www.randomhouse.com/teachers

Library of Congress Cataloging-in-Publication Data
Wollman, Jessica.
Second skin / Jessica Wollman.—1st ed.
p.   cm.
Summary: Despite the consequences, sophomore Samantha Klein pursues her dream of becoming popular at Woodlawn High School.
ISBN 978-0-385-73601-5 (trade pbk.)—ISBN 978-0-375-89259-2 (e-book)
[1. Popularity—Fiction. 2. High schools—Fiction. 3. Schools—Fiction.]
I. Title.
PZ7.W8355Se 2009
[Fic]—dc22   2008044861

The text of this book is set in 11.5-point Base Twelve Serif.
Book design by Cathy Boback.

Printed in the United States of America

10 9 8 7 6 5 4 3 2 1

First Edition

for Paulina

Many many thanks to . . .

Wendy Loggia, Krista Vitola, Marci Senders
and the whole team at Delacorte Press
for all their hard work.
Richard Abate for making this book happen.
Caroline Wallace for the lovely photo.
My family for all their support.
And especially to Dan—for everything.

SECOND SKIN

Popularity is the one insult
I have never suffered.

—Oscar Wilde

How it begins . . .

It arrives mysteriously, under your pillow.
A small package and a set of rules.
There is confusion, of course, but it doesn't last.
The promise of what's to come is much
too powerful, too enticing.

This is a gift that's never returned.

Because, in the end, everyone wants it:
the young, the old and the in-between.
The want is universal.
And the supply is extremely limited.

So if you've been chosen,
consider yourself lucky.
But be careful, too.
This is one high-maintenance item.
And sometimes what we want
is the absolute worst thing for us.

ONE

Do I remember how it happened? Of course I do. Going from total and complete loser to all-out social goddess in a matter of days just isn't the sort of thing anyone forgets. I don't care how busy you are. But it wasn't like I planned this, either. Well, not really.

What you need to remember is this: I wanted to be popular.

I know that's not a very original desire. It's about as cutting-edge as asking your parents for a car on your sixteenth birthday. Still, it's important for you to know, right from the start: I never wanted to mess up anybody's life. And I definitely never wanted anyone to get hurt.

I just wanted to be popular.

Unfortunately for me and almost everyone I know, my desire caused a lot of problems.

Major problems.

Homeroom was the real trigger. Until last spring, it was also my favorite class.

I realize that sounds a little weird. I mean, what's there to love about homeroom, right? It's twenty minutes of lame announcements and roll call. Come to think of it, I'm not even sure homeroom *is* a class, since school doesn't officially start until after it ends.

Whatever. I said it *used* to be my favorite. Past tense. As in: it's not anymore.

Besides, my reasons for loving homeroom had nothing to do with attendance sheets or cafeteria menus. I don't even buy my lunch. (Two years ago my mother read a *Newsweek* article about the "evil" business behind America's school lunch programs. I've been brown-bagging it ever since. I'm not really sure how my not eating frozen pizza is going to bankrupt Kraft Foods, but I do know that arguing with my mom is a complete waste of time. My sloppy joe days are definitely over.) And I pretty much tuned out my teacher, Mr. Martino, once he checked my name off the roll.

For me, it was really a matter of real estate.

Homeroom seats were assigned alphabetically the first day of freshman year. Unless you changed your last name, you weren't allowed to move, no matter what. You pretty much kept the same desk until you graduated.

That's how I, Samantha Klein, wound up sitting between Ella Murphy and Jules Johnston for twenty minutes each day Monday through Friday.

I know those names don't mean anything to you, but believe me, if you attended Woodlawn High School, they would.

I was smack in the middle of an A-list district.

That's why I wished homeroom were three times longer. It was the only time of day I felt mildly cool.

Okay, maybe that's pushing it. Just so you know, I wasn't exactly designed with "cool" in mind. No matter where I sat, I'd still have the same fat, curly hair that makes me look like I'm holding one of those static-electricity balls we used to play with at the Please Touch Museum. And my skin's guaranteed to keep Neutrogena in business for the next century.

Alphabetical order can only do so much.

But as of last spring, those twenty minutes were the closest I'd ever gotten to high school. Not my lame version of high school—the one with the honor-roll grades and the Kate Hudson movie marathon nights—but the high school I knew other people attended. People like Ella and Jules. The high school with tons of friends, hot boyfriends (personally, I'd have settled for just one . . . but the hot part was definitely *not* negotiable) and invites to all those cool parties . . . parties with no parents and drunken skinny-dipping and who knows what else because I spent my weekends babysitting.

Since I never spoke to anyone sitting around me, I used homeroom to perfect my eavesdropping skills. So when Jules and Ella started up that morning right after Christmas break, I had no trouble following along.

"She broke up with him?" Ella asked as she slid into her chair. She had the sort of pale skin that responded to everything with a deep flush. Staring at her, I could almost feel the red as it spread across her cheeks. "Are you sure?"

"I can't believe you're surprised." Jules pulled a lip gloss from her bag and twisted off the top. "I totally saw this coming. I didn't even think they'd make it to Saturday."

"But Matt's so great."

I knew right away they were talking about Kylie Frank.

Everyone was always talking about Kylie Frank.

"He's fine, I guess. But Tanner's better," Jules

was saying. Even though my desk was wedged in right next to hers, she always talked right through me, as if I weren't there.

And I wasn't. Not to the Jules Johnstons of the world.

I didn't mind, though. Not really. The whole invisible thing worked both ways. For instance, at that very moment, I was staring directly at her, waiting for her to continue. I didn't even bother to open a notebook and pretend to read.

Sometimes being nobody really comes in handy.

Overnight Jules's hair had changed color. The day before it had been wheat blond, but this morning it was more of a butterscotch.

This was pretty typical. In a hopeless attempt to match Kylie Frank's glossy yellow locks, Jules hopped from shade to shade on an almost weekly basis. Every time I passed the Clairol aisle in the drugstore, I thought of her. Honeysuckle, Silent Snow, Bold Gold . . . Jules had tried them all. The girl just couldn't leave her hair alone.

"I mean, I can totally see why she did it," she whispered.

A smirk crowded Ella's tiny features. "Of course you can."

"What's *that* supposed to mean?" Annoyed,

Jules flipped her hair. I watched, fascinated, as the painted strands fell obediently back into place.

Ella's face puckered as she swallowed a giggle.

Not that my opinion really mattered, but I had to side with Jules on this one. Matt Kane was cute, but Tanner Mullins? Forget it. He was easily the best-looking guy at Woodlawn. He didn't belong in high school; he belonged on a billboard. I couldn't have designed a hotter guy.

And now he was dating Kylie Frank. Of course. It was a perfect match between two perfect people. They'd probably get married and live someplace . . . perfect.

I was pretty sure I'd end up marrying my cat. Not that I had a cat, but I figured it was only a matter of time.

"Whoa. I can't believe how close we cut it this morning."

As Kylie Frank slid into the desk directly in front of mine, I watched the entire room respond to her entrance. There were sly glances, eager waves and studied nonchalance. Everyone contributed their own special something.

Not that Kylie noticed. That was one of the things that set her apart from other A-listers, like Jules. So many of them walked around as if they were being filmed for a new MTV pilot.

Watching them, you could almost hear the voice-over: *This is my locker . . . see all the pictures of my friends? We have so much fun together.*

Kylie wasn't like that. She just wasn't at all self-conscious. She really seemed to have absolutely no clue that she had the power to change everything. All she had to do was show up.

Whatever "it" was, Kylie Frank had been dealt an unfair amount. I was pretty sure she'd been given my portion, too. How else could you explain it? Even though we were the same age, Kylie seemed older than I could ever be. Or feel. I was sure that at fifty, pictures of a sixteen-year-old Kylie Frank would still make me feel hopelessly immature.

Or maybe just plain hopeless.

This morning was no exception. As usual, Kylie's buttery hair poured down her back, so shiny that, under the cheap fluorescent lights, it looked almost laminated. Her flawless, peachy skin was a facialist's dream. And she looked absolutely perfect in a pair of skinny jeans and pony-skin flats. Her square-necked tunic framed her thin, toned shoulders as if the cloth had been lowered over her head and cut specifically to her body.

That was another thing: Kylie Frank could wear anything. Like everything else, clothing loved her. The girl was living proof that natural beauty did exist; not everyone had to work hard to look perfect.

Glancing down at my no-name brown cords and canvas high-tops, I felt a twinge of regret. My dad's a labor lawyer who thinks that all chain stores are Satan. If you even whisper the words "Abercrombie and Fitch," he throws a *fit*. Before anyone in my family shops at a new store, he researches it, just to be sure the owners are union-friendly and practice equal opportunity employment.

It's not like I don't believe in fair labor practices. I do. But every once in a while it'd be really nice to buy a sweater at the mall like a normal person.

Jules leaned across the aisle and placed a possessive hand on Kylie's arm. All signs of strain were completely erased from her face.

"*We?*" she said, smiling coyly. "Interesting. Very interesting."

Kylie cast a guilty look in Ella's direction. "Well, Tanner gave me a ride. It was on his way."

Jules giggled. "*Right.* He's so into you."

Ella's eyebrows met. "What about Matt? You know, he really likes you."

Kylie ran a hand through her hair. I wondered what it was like to have hair that slipped right through your fingers. The sort of hair that actually grows down, not out. Mine's so frizzy it feels like Brillo when I touch it.

"Matt's sweet," Kylie said. "But I think we're better as friends."

Ella shook her head and it suddenly occurred to me—I'd never even considered it before—that she might not be enjoying Kylie's royal status. She didn't look jealous, though. She looked worried.

"I totally called this," Jules crowed. She turned to Ella, triumphant. "Didn't I call this?"

"You sure did."

Kylie sighed. "Stop it, okay, Ellie? Don't make me feel bad. I can see anyone I want."

"Of course you can, sweetie." Jules was practically glowing. She was always looking for ways to strip Ella of her "Kylie's closest friend" status. But even I knew this was a losing battle. Kylie and Ella had gone to the same grade school and had been best friends since kindergarten. And although Jules was indulged, Kylie seemed to hold her at a distance. But her voice—whether consciously or not—always warmed whenever she spoke to Ella.

"It's just—I don't know." Ella hesitated for only a second. "Tanner seems—"

Jules's eyebrows shot up. "Hot? Cool? Sexy?"

"Wait, isn't that the name of a Red Hot Chili Peppers album?" Kylie asked.

Jules gloated, confident she was just a split end away from having Kylie all to herself.

"Limited. Tanner seems limited," Ella continued, ignoring them both. Her lips dipped into a frown. "Look, do what you want, definitely. But don't you think you should make sure Matt's okay?"

"Why bother?" Jules snorted. "He saw you and Tanner talking last week. He's probably figured it out by now."

Kylie opened her mouth to say something then seemed to change her mind. "No, Ella's right. I should call him."

Jules's hand curled into a tight fist as her eyes flashed over Ella's skirt. "There should really be a law banning Jones New York for anyone under forty," she muttered, though I'm pretty sure I was the only one who heard her. When she spoke again, her voice was sweet and faux casual. "Sure. No biggie."

Kylie smiled easily. "I'll do it tomorrow night, after the move. Tonight's gonna be crazy."

"How about I come over and help?" Jules offered quickly, sniffing out another opportunity. "It'll be fun."

"Thanks, but you so don't want to go there. Everything's such a mess." Kylie's smile lit her sapphire eyes, making them glitter. "But you guys have to check out the new place, over on

Thorncrest. My parents combined two of the upstairs bedrooms for me, so my room's gigantic . . . plus I get my own bathroom. . . ."

The morning bell sounded, drowning out the rest of Kylie's sentence. I didn't care, though. I wasn't even listening. I was miles away, standing in front of my house at 176 Thorncrest Drive. It's pretty much your typical suburban home: white brick, split-level, clean lawn. Not the sort of place you'd see in *Architectural Digest*.

But here's the thrilling part: turning just a half step to the left, I was now facing a large, empty redbrick house with a FOR SALE/SOLD! sign in the front yard—178 Thorncrest Drive.

My pulse quickened.

Kylie Frank—*the* Kylie Frank—was my new neighbor.

TWO

"So wait. This affects you how?"

All morning long, I'd been dying to share the big news with my best friends, Gwen Connolly and Alex Ashby, but now I felt stupid for getting so excited.

"It doesn't," I said in my best I-so-don't-care voice. "It's just nice to have a new neighbor."

We were sitting at our usual lunch table, toward the front of the cafeteria. I watched as Gwen carefully unwrapped her latest culinary masterpiece, a peanut-butter-swirl chocolate brownie. As usual, her thick brown hair was pulled into a messy, thoughtless ponytail, and she wore her self-described "chubby girl uniform": wide-leg pants with an elastic waistband—not quite sweatpants but definitely not pants pants—and an oversized sweater that grazed her knees. All black, of course. Gwen always joked that once a girl reached a certain weight, the fashion world closed the box of Crayolas on her. If she dressed in any shade lighter than charcoal, the plus-size police would track her down and haul her off to a carb-free jail.

"Yum." She sank her teeth into the dense chocolate and swallowed. "Definitely beats last week's meringues. It's always best to go classic."

I pulled my own lunch from a recycled brown bag. Besides Gwen, whose refined palate couldn't handle frozen lasagna and Oodles of Noodles, I was probably the only kid at Woodlawn who didn't eat the crappy cafeteria food.

I sniffed my sandwich and dropped it onto the table. The only thing lamer than a bag lunch is a bag lunch containing tofu bologna.

"Want some?" Alex pushed his bowl of mac and cheese in my direction, spoon extended.

"Thanks," I said, grateful.

"I can see how it might be cool to have someone new move in," Alex mused, backing me up. "Everyone on my street's over eighty. I keep telling my mom we should open a Denny's."

I laughed, then covered my mouth, which was full of pasta.

Gwen rolled her eyes. "Sure, having a new neighbor's great. Except when she happens to be the Wicked Witch of the West." She used her index finger to mop up some stray brownie crumbs. "Post–Zone diet."

This was nothing new. To Gwen, all A-listers looked mean and disgustingly malnourished. A serious foodie, she spent most of her free time perfecting her soufflé and dreaming of the French Culinary Institute. By the third week of school freshman year, she was already counting the days until graduation. She hated Woodlawn. Of course, she claimed that *it* hated *her* first, but at this point it didn't really matter who'd started it up. She was definitely holding a grudge.

"Come on," I said. "You don't even know her."

As if on cue, the three of us turned our heads toward the back of the cafeteria, where Tanner Mullins was trying to pull a shrieking Kylie onto his lap. Everyone around them was laughing as if it were the funniest thing they'd ever seen.

Gwen snorted. "Believe me. I know enough."

It was useless. I loved my friends. They were great—so smart and funny—but they were completely closed off to all things high school. Gwen was practically married to her kitchen, and Alex was always developing some strange new interest that had nothing to do with school, like building soapbox cars in his garage or discovering comets from his roof. Even though he got straight As, he'd never join the debate team or computer club. School activities just didn't occur to him.

And neither Gwen nor Alex ever thought about their nonexistent social lives. They embraced their fringe/loser status as if it weren't at all important.

This *killed* me.

Okay, so maybe people hassled Gwen about her weight. They called her Pot Roast Connolly and made fun of her 36DD chest. It was totally rude, but did she have to write off *all* of high school just because football players were jerks? And Alex actually looked sort of cute when he remembered to cut his hair and change his T-shirt. Couldn't they try to be a little more upbeat? It was only sophomore year.

I watched as Tanner pretended to pour a Red Bull over Kylie's head. She was leaning back, her face tilted up to the ceiling. Her hair tumbled down her back in a long yellow free fall, loose and natural.

How could anyone not want to be a part of that? I wondered.

It just wasn't fair. I would've done anything to have Tanner Mullins pour a Red Bull over my head. He could've poured a whole case of Red Bulls. I'd have paid him to do it. I'd even pay for the Red Bulls, too.

Alex nudged me with his elbow. "You're drooling, you know."

I turned my head and blinked. "Wait, what?"

Alex got a weird look on his face, like he'd just eaten something really sour. "You know. Tanner Mullins, all-star male bimbo. You're practically foaming at the mouth." He sounded impatient, almost annoyed.

Gwen looked at us and groaned. "Come on," she said to me. "You should be happy you're not over there, Sam. You're way too cool."

"Here it comes." Alex shook his head but he was smiling now. His voice sounded relaxed.

I shot my hand up in mock protest, relieved that his tone had lightened. "No! I take it all back, okay? Just no theory. *Please.*"

Last year, after a particularly humiliating gym class starring Gwen and a very broken sports bra, she'd formed a simple theory about the four years commonly referred to as high school but which she called hell. The theory, she claimed, was grounded in fact and based on extensive research (personal experience in the form of cruel gags and snide remarks). Basically, it went something like this: high school is stupid.

Following this logic, any truly cool person could never ever be appreciated at Woodlawn. Similarly, everyone at the top of the food chain was completely soulless and moronic.

Convinced her theory was genius, Gwen invoked it at every opportunity. Alex and I had heard the same lecture so many times that just mentioning it made us laugh.

"For your information," Gwen announced, "I wasn't even thinking about that." She smiled grandly. "But now that you mention it . . ."

I giggled as Alex made fake vomiting noises.

But to be honest, my heart wasn't really in it. A part of me was already walking to the back of the cafeteria, ready to join Tanner and Kylie and the Red Bull. A part of me had already decided.

I was going to find a way in. I'd make it work. Kylie's move *was* the best thing that could've happened to me.

I'd show them.

THREE

Okay. I might not be cool. I might have fusilli hair. I might have only two friends and—thanks to my consumer-culture-hating parents and their no-brand-name leanings—be saddled with a wardrobe that would traumatize Marc Jacobs.

But I, Samantha Klein, could sure put together a killer gift basket.

When I got home from school that afternoon, the moving vans were parked in Kylie's new driveway. For two solid hours I watched as furniture and boxes were lugged into the big brick house.

As soon as things calmed down, I got to work.

It was all a part of my new carpe diem attitude: only Samantha Klein could make things happen for Samantha Klein.

Project gift basket was my first take-charge move. And phase one of the plan—putting together the actual basket—was simple. A little tissue paper, some of Gwen's gourmet brownies and a big Welcome! card purchased at one of those fancy stationery stores my mother despised, and I was in business. No problem.

Phase two, however, was a little more difficult. Said gift basket had to be given. This meant that I had to actually visit the most popular girl in school. At her house. Completely uninvited.

This was why I found myself standing on Kylie Frank's new front porch admiring the bounty I was supposed to be delivering but absolutely unable to deliver it.

Just raise your hand, I kept telling myself. *Knock. Ring. Yell. Do something.*

I lifted my arm but hesitated when I read my watch. It was seven. What if the Franks were eating dinner? Or what if they hated unexpected guests, even ones bearing dessert?

Maybe it was best to leave the gift on the porch.

I tried to lower the basket to the floor but this voice—this *really annoying* voice—started to swirl around inside my head.

No. Carpe diem. You have to do this. Now.

So before I lost my nerve again—and to shut the voice up—I leaned forward and pushed the bell. I could hear the chime as it rang through the house.

A pretty blond woman opened the door. She was holding a wad of bills. She had really smooth skin and familiar sapphire eyes. Even though she was wearing jeans and an old T-shirt, I could tell just by looking at her that she had a closet filled with all sorts of amazing designers, the sort of clothing that in my house triggered a three-hour lecture on the evils of an industry built on hyperinflated markups and a flagrant disregard for animal rights.

This was definitely Kylie Frank's mother.

Not once during my many months of eavesdropping had I ever wondered about Kylie Frank's family. It was sort of hard to believe she even had a family. Not in an orphan sort of way. There were just certain people who seemed beyond parents and all the things they represented, like allowance and curfews and corny jokes.

Kylie Frank was definitely one of those people.

"You're not my moo shu pork," the woman said. She sounded surprised and not at all pleased. When she spoke again, her voice was cold and definite. "Kylie isn't allowed to have friends over on school nights. Different house, same rules."

Despite her tone, I couldn't help feeling a little flattered. Flattered and shocked. I stared at Mrs. Frank. Did she actually think I was one of her daughter's friends? Was she blind? Kylie's friends were cute and fashionable. They wore Juicy Couture and Paige Premium . . . and looked great.

I wore . . . no one. And didn't.

I tried again. "Uh, no. I'm not a friend—I mean . . . I'm actually your new neighbor. Sam Klein." I thrust the gift into Mrs. Frank's arms a little harder than I should have. One of the brownies slid over the side of the basket and flopped to the floor. "Welcome to Thorncrest," I mumbled lamely.

Mrs. Frank stepped out onto the porch and picked up the squashed brownie. When she straightened, her expression had warmed. "Oh! How sweet!"

Is Kylie even home? I wondered. *Maybe she's out with Tanner?*

The door swung open again and I held my breath. A dark-haired man who definitely wasn't Kylie filled the doorway.

I was relieved. Extremely relieved.

But just a little disappointed, too.

25

He smiled at me. "Who's this?"

"Honey, meet our new neighbor, Sam Klein." Kylie's mom lifted the basket. "Look, she brought us a housewarming gift. Isn't that nice?" She turned back to me. "I'm Lydia Frank and this is my husband, George."

Without thinking, I extended my hand, hesitating midlift. Was it weird to shake now? I never knew.

Luckily, Mr. Frank took the cue. "It's very nice to meet you, Sam Klein," he said in that jokey-dad sort of way. He gestured to the neighboring houses. "So which one is yours?"

I pointed awkwardly to the left. My body just didn't seem to be moving properly. "Uh, my parents wanted to come too. They're working late."

Now, why had I said that? My dad's car was in the driveway, mere yards away. Both my parents were at home, watching Jim Lehrer. If they'd known what I was doing, they'd have insisted on coming over too. Just picturing my mother in her harem pants and felt clogs, lecturing Kylie's parents on the benefits of green living, made me feel faint.

"Oh, well. Another time," Mrs. Frank said. "I'm sorry if I was rude before." She looked at her husband. "I thought she was here for Kylie."

"Oh, don't worry about it," I said quickly, hoping to avoid the inevitable. But Mrs. Frank was already studying me, her blue eyes sharp with realization.

"Say, what school do you go to?" she asked.

Great. What was I supposed to do now? If I mentioned Woodlawn, they'd definitely ask if I knew Kylie. And any sort of admission would trigger a similar conversation with their daughter. I could just see the whole humiliating scene play out. I could feel Kylie's confusion as she sifted through a mental yearbook, searching for my face . . . only to come up empty-handed.

"Our daughter's about your age," Mrs. Frank was explaining. She turned toward the house. "You two should definitely meet. Kylie! *Kylie!*"

Panic ripped through me. The porch started to spin.

Abort. Abort mission.

I couldn't do this. Not yet.

Forget carpe diem. I had to go home.

Kylie's mother frowned. "She was upstairs just a minute ago. She might be on the phone."

"Uh, that's okay. I should really—"

"Chinese food?"

The delivery guy from A Wok on the Wild Side had a serious unibrow and was in desperate need of a training bra. Still, I felt like kissing him.

"Listen," I said, turning toward the steps, "I'll let you guys eat. It was really nice to meet you."

"Are you sure you don't want to stay for some

egg rolls?" Kylie's father asked as he reached out to grab the order.

"No, that's okay. Thanks, though." I flashed Kylie's parents my first genuine smile of the entire conversation. It was hard not to sprint as I stepped off the porch.

"Thanks for the gift!" Mr. Frank called after me. His head was half buried in the take-out bag and his voice was muffled.

As I walked back to my house, I could hear Mrs. Frank calling Kylie.

Everyone was always calling Kylie Frank.

FOUR

The next morning I tried again.

Baby steps, I told myself as I sat in homeroom waiting for the A-listers to fill the chairs around me. Last night I'd been too ambitious—had expected too much. That's why I'd freaked out. What had I been thinking? That after a bite of brownie Kylie Frank would suddenly open her eyes and decide she was desperately in need of a frizzy-haired friend who knew way too much about hemp? It was ridiculous.

I had to manage my expectations. Overnight, I'd streamlined my plan. Instant change wasn't realistic. But small, simple goals—*that* I could

29

handle. Maybe I wouldn't leap from F- to A-list, but I might just manage to creep.

Today's assignment? Make conversation—*talk* to Kylie Frank. It didn't have to be anything deep—no debates on capital punishment or where she saw herself in fifteen years—but it had to be an actual exchange. I kept reminding myself that "Is this your pen?" or "Excuse me but you're standing on my foot" wouldn't cut it.

I'm going to do it, I thought. *We're neighbors now. There's a lot we can talk about. Besides, Kylie Frank's just a person. How hard can it be?*

As if on cue, Kylie floated into the room, followed by Jules and Ella. She was stunning in a fitted black leather jacket, leopard-print leggings and metallic flats. It was sort of amazing how the outfit was so chic on her but, I had no doubt, would make me look like an escapee from a mental hospital.

"It's gonna be great," Jules was saying. "I can't believe they're gonna be away for the whole weekend."

Kylie slid into her desk, dropping her black patent-leather bag onto the floor. "I know," she said, twisting around to face her friends. "My mom almost canceled since there's still so much unpacking to do, but my dad said they'd lose their deposit, so . . ." She trailed off, smiling widely. "Off they go!"

"I don't know," Ella said, chewing her lower lip. "You *just* moved. Those parties can get pretty out of control. Remember what happened at Gina's?"

I shuddered. Even I'd heard about Gina Yonas's wild party and—thanks to a very clogged downstairs toilet—her never to be white again wall-to-wall carpeting.

"It's fine," Kylie said quickly, but I'd seen the shadow pass over her face. "We have hardwood floors."

"Besides, Gina let everyone in," Jules quipped, shooting Ella a "you're so hopeless" look. "We're gonna have a guest list."

"Right," Kylie agreed, flipping open her iPhone. "Just a few people—it'll be intimate. Very chic."

Ella shrugged, but she still looked concerned.

So Kylie Frank was planning a party. An A-list soiree was being thrown less than a hundred yards from my own bedroom.

Not that I'd be invited. At least, not today. But if I worked hard and stuck to the plan, it wasn't completely out of the question.

First things first, I thought, straightening slightly. If I wanted an invite—or anything else A-list—I'd have to *talk* to the A-listers first.

"Tanner's gonna want beer," Ella warned. "There's nothing chic about a keg."

"Oh, quit being so negative," Jules huffed. "So we have a keg. Big deal. Bob's Beverage doesn't card. We can get one from there."

"It's closed," I blurted out, remembering an article in the paper bearing a headline to the tune of LOCAL DISTRIBUTOR CLOSED FOR SALES TO TODDLERS.

I lifted my head. Ella, Jules and Kylie were staring at me. Arched eyebrows framed their surprised expressions.

Jules was the first to recover. "Please. Like *you* know anything about buying a keg."

I felt the color swirl into my cheeks. *Just ignore her,* I thought. *This isn't perfect, but at least you have their attention.*

I looked at Kylie and forced myself to smile. "Um, you just moved next door to me," I told her. "On Thorncrest. I'm Sam. I live in the, uh, white house."

"Great," Kylie said, her voice flat as she studied her French manicure.

An awkward silence descended. It only lasted for a few seconds, but it was just long enough for me to imagine throwing a chair then myself through the nearest window.

"Um, if you have questions about the neighborhood or anything," I said, pushing on. "Just ask."

"Thanks," Kylie said, her eyes still on her nails. "But I think I can handle it."

The bell rang as Mr. Martino rushed into the room, roll book in hand.

I watched as Kylie dropped her iPhone back into her bag, then turned to face forward.

Jules pouted. "Great. Now we don't have time for the guest list." She scowled at me. "Next time, try your own conversation?"

"Whatever," Kylie said, without turning. She still sounded bored. "We can figure it out during lunch."

I studied the back of her head, wondering if she had—in a weird way—just defended me.

Okay, maybe that was a stretch. But at least I'd made some progress on my plan. On the other hand, I wasn't sure if my reception—a bunch of not-so-veiled insults—really counted as progress.

Forget baby steps, I thought, sliding down in my chair. *I'd settle for a crawl.*

FIVE

"Um, what's that smell?" I shrugged off my coat and looked around my living room.

Wait, *was* this my living room? It used to be. This morning, when I left for school, it had been. Now it looked more like a chemistry lab. In less than six hours, the furniture had been pushed up against the walls, and the floor was covered with all sorts of buckets and large white jugs.

And the whole place reeked of . . . salad dressing?

"Hi, sweetie!" My mom looked up at me from

her cross-legged position on the floor. "How was your day?"

I clamped my hand over my nose. "Fine. What's going on?"

My mom untangled her legs and stood, wiping her hands on her navy sweatpants. "I'm green cleaning the house," she announced importantly. She grabbed one of the jugs and gave it a dramatic little shake. "Vinegar."

"Neat," I said, completely unenthusiastic. I didn't ask for more information. Like it or not, I knew more was coming.

"I've always hated the idea of showering the house with toxic commercial cleaners," my mother continued, as if she were being interviewed on the *Today* show. She pointed an accusing finger at a big crate in the corner stuffed with bottles of Windex and Comet. "All those chemicals are petroleum-based."

I nodded, pretending to be intimately acquainted with the evils of petroleum and all its bases. The information was probably in one of the many articles my mother taped to my door on a daily basis with a "Sam—MUST read!!!" Post-it attached.

It's not like I tossed the articles out or anything. I mean, I definitely intended to read them. One day. In the meantime, I kept them stacked in my closet next to a box filled with my old Halloween costumes.

"Philadelphia—well, the entire East Coast, actually—is just so behind the times," my mother said mournfully, placing her hands on her hips. "Did you know that San Francisco has entire cleaning crews that'll green your house for you?"

In the interest of ending the ecolecture as quickly as possible, I tried to make a face that communicated my outrage at this coast's addiction to lemon Pledge.

"It really is amazing what you can do with baking soda and a little vinegar," my mother marveled. "And it's incredibly cost-efficient too. I should've done this years ago."

My mom's a part-time accountant for Greenpeace's Philly office. I guess Greenpeace is the sort of place where even the number crunchers are passionate about the cause.

I never told either of my parents this, but sometimes I wished they had jobs that were just jobs, not causes. Gwen's dad was a dentist but he never lectured us about WaterPiks or railed against the perils of unflossed gums. And when he watched the news, that's all he did. Watched. He didn't shout things at the television or write angry letters to the anchors.

It's a miracle that Katie Couric never took out a restraining order against my parents.

"So, wanna help me mix?" my mother asked brightly. "We can have a little green party down here."

Oh god. Did my mom just say "green party"?

She reached down and grabbed a felt bag with the words *I Am Not a Plastic Bag* stamped across the front. "And here are some pamphlets about the whole 'Go Green, Stay Clean' movement. I thought you'd want to take them to school. I'm sure the custodial staff would be really interested."

I felt my stomach clench. For the record, I've never had anything against the environment. Or stuffing my house with *I Am Not a Plastic Bag* bags. I was even pretty sure that, once my sinuses cleared, I'd get used to living in a bottle of vinaigrette. But home and school are two very different ecosystems.

I pointed at the offending felt. "I'm not taking that to school."

"Of course not," my mother said, laughing as if I'd just told her the most hilarious joke. "I'll get you a smaller bag. This one's huge."

I opened my mouth to protest, then realized the situation was hopeless. Not just because my mother was impossible to argue with, but because if I refused she'd probably just visit the school herself. And that would be way worse than, um, anything.

Couldn't I just be a *closeted* green person?

I wondered if the felt bags could be ordered with personalized statements printed on them. *Sam Klein Is a Hopeless Loser* sounded just about right.

"Forget it," I muttered. "Did I get any mail?"

"Just another one of your vapid magazines," my mother said, disapproval dripping from her voice. "*Elle* or something?" She sighed. "I really wish you'd consider reading that was a little more . . . inspiring."

"*Elle is* inspiring," I defended. "Every time I read, I'm inspired to buy a new pair of jeans or get my bangs cut."

My mother shook her head mournfully, as if I'd just presented her with a lifetime membership to the NRA.

"There's a whole world out there that has absolutely nothing to do with fashion tips and the red carpet," she informed me.

I looked around the room, at the green felt bags and the framed—yes, framed—Greenpeace posters hanging on the walls (MAY THE FOREST BE WITH YOU and SAVE OUR PLANET FROM CORPORATE GREED).

"No kidding," I muttered, turning toward the steps. "Listen, I have a ton of work to do."

I stomped up to my room and shut the door with just a little more force than was absolutely necessary. After a minute, though, I started to feel sort of bad. It really wasn't my mother's fault I was in such a bad mood.

It was Kylie Frank's.

Three weeks. Twenty-one days and, according to my calculator, 504 hours. That was how long it had been since the most popular girl in several zip codes moved in next door to me. And in that time, guess what had happened?

Nothing. Absolutely nothing. At least to me. Kylie Frank, on the other hand, was extremely busy leading her ultrafabulous A-list life.

She was definitely too busy to meet her F-list neighbor, Sam Klein.

It's not like I didn't try. I'd plowed ahead with the baby-steps plan. I'd tried brownies, light chatter and the occasional hanging out in my front yard, with the hopes of triggering a "spontaneous" Kylie Frank run-in.

Nothing worked. Food bribes and banter might've won over Kylie's parents—they always waved and smiled when I saw them—but Kylie was impervious. Or maybe not impervious, just never around.

That was the real problem. The girl used her new house to sleep and change clothes, nothing more. I knew this because, even though I hadn't gotten to know her at all, I'd definitely learned a lot *about* her.

For instance, she left for school every morning at around eight-fifteen (and by "leave," I mean she hopped into Tanner Mullins's red Mustang convertible and the two sped off, happily fabulous). She didn't blow her hair dry either. (Oddly, this was the aspect of Kylie's life that drove me most crazy. *How* could you have hair that perfect *naturally*? If life were even remotely fair, Kylie would have flatirons instead of hands.) On weeknights, she got home around eight, driven by Tanner, Jules or Ella.

And don't get me started on the weekends. That was another completely depressing (for me) story.

At first, I tried to stay positive about the whole thing. I told myself that with so much popularity in such close range, some of it was bound to rub off. I didn't need actual contact with Kylie; I could learn through observation alone.

I spent three days watching her float around (have you ever noticed how It-girls don't walk?), memorizing her graceful moves. I really thought I had it down, too. And then I got to school and walked right into a pole. And I mean smacked into the thing. (Really, what sort of idiot architect places a pole in the middle of a school hallway? No wonder everyone's always complaining about the state of public education.) I grew a second head for almost a week.

And this morning, I woke up at five-thirty to blow out my hair—long, sleek and straight, just like Kylie's. I thought I did a pretty good job, too.

And then Gwen picked me up.

"What's with the hair?" she asked, twisting around in the driver's seat to open the back door. For some really weird reason, Doug, Gwen's ten-year-old Dodge Neon, only responded to her touch. Whenever anyone else jiggled the handles, the doors stayed stubbornly shut.

Alex and I kept telling her this was a major safety hazard, but Gwen insisted that the car was just being loyal. Like a Dalmatian.

"What do you mean?" I asked, raising a hand defensively to my head. It was definitely straighter than usual, but it felt pretty sticky from the half bottle of "smoothing cream" I'd used. And it was still pretty rough, too. Definitely more burlap than silk. Or burlap with a dab of peanut butter spread over it.

As I climbed into the backseat, Alex dropped his *Ant-Man* comic and turned around to look at me.

"Ginger has a purse just like that," he said, pointing to my hair. Ginger is Alex's four-year-old sister. "I think it's called faux fur?"

Gwen burst out laughing.

"You guys suck," I said, sinking back against the seat cushion. So much for popularity of the DIY variety. "Does anyone have a rubber band?"

That was my morning. And nothing. Happened. All day. And now it was Friday night. I was heading into a weekend where the most exciting thing I had planned was babysitting the Packler twins, Bella and Grace.

Even so, I couldn't stop the excitement from building. It came every Friday, curling through me with absolutely no release. And when I woke up on Saturday morning, I felt completely depressed. My weekends were like sinking your teeth into wax fruit.

There was a whole part of life that I wasn't living.

The A-listers were living it for me.

I groaned. I was sort of tempted to bail, but Mr. and Mrs. Packler were really nice, and they'd never find a replacement so last-minute. Besides, I really didn't have anything better to do. By now, Gwen was probably whipping up a cheesecake, and Alex spent most nights up on his roof staring through his telescope.

I might as well get paid for watching *The Frog Princess.*

Actually, I thought, *maybe I should take notes. I might pick up a few pointers.*

SIX

When I woke up the next morning, Alex was sitting at my kitchen table, sandwiched between my parents. There was a huge stack of whole wheat pancakes in front of him.

"What are you doing here?" I asked, suddenly aware that I was still wearing my too-small SAVE THE DUGONG nightshirt.

As if he'd just read my mind, Alex pointed at my chest and smiled. "The dugong. Cousin of the manatee. Glad to know you're a fan."

My parents beamed at him like he'd just shrunk their carbon footprints.

I tried again. "It's Saturday." I watched Alex

scoop up more pancake pieces and shovel them into his mouth. When he didn't answer, I added, "We don't have school."

"It's a good thing too," he said, wiping his hands on a napkin. He pushed his chair back and stood. "This isn't just any Saturday."

"It's not?"

"No way." He paused for dramatic effect. When he spoke again, his voice was announcer-low. "It's your quarter birthday."

I laughed. "My *what*?"

"You're sixteen-point-two-five years old today, Sam," Alex announced. His thick dark hair, still wet from the shower, stuck up in little tufts around his head. "It's an unsung milestone in every girl's life."

I grinned and slid into an empty chair. "And here I was, worried you'd forget."

Alex's mouth fell open. "No way. *I'm* a friend."

"I still remember *my* sixteen-and-a-quarter birthday," my mother said, faux wistfully. "It was magical."

My dad lowered his paper and rolled his eyes. "You people are crazy," he said, but he sounded amused.

Alex lifted his fork. "Big plans today, Sam. Huge."

I stood, giving my nightshirt a quick tug. "Okay, let me just go get changed."

"Hurry!" Alex shouted as I scrambled up the stairs. "Once you hit point-two-six it's all over!"

I hopped into the shower. For the first time in a week, I actually felt excited about something that had absolutely nothing to do with Kylie Frank.

It felt good. I needed a little vacation.

Drying off, I slipped into a pair of jeans and a plain, no-message T-shirt and ran back downstairs. Alex was waiting for me at the door.

"Just drive carefully," my mother shouted after us as we left.

Alex looked at me knowingly. "She's right," he said. "*Lots* of accidents associated with the quarter birthday."

We headed out to his car, a dark blue station wagon he'd rebuilt so many times I doubted any of the original parts still existed. As I yanked the door open, my gaze shifted next door. The curtains to Kylie's room were still drawn. She was probably sleeping off the aftereffects of a crazy night.

I'd returned from the Packlers' at ten-thirty, covered with finger paint and graham cracker crumbs, and was fast asleep by eleven.

I shoved the thought out of my head and turned to Alex.

"So," I said, slipping my arm through the seat belt. "Where are we going?"

He pursed his lips and tried to look mysterious. "It's a surprise."

"Can I guess?"

"You can try," he said as he eased the car out of the driveway. "But you'll never get it."

"Um, Cape May?"

Alex's face fell. "How did you— Did Gwen say something?"

I laughed. "Lucky guess."

I tilted my head back against the seat. It was January and cold, but the sun was up and it streamed through the car windows, warm and relaxing. I stretched, turning to Alex. "Hey, maybe we should stop by Gwen's and pick her up."

"She's busy," he said a little too quickly.

I sighed. I hated tension between my friends. "Don't be mad," I told him. "She didn't tell, I swear."

"I know." He stuck an arm out of the window, signaling a turn. "But I talked to her last night. She was all excited about going to Reading Terminal. I guess rhubarb's finally in season."

That made sense. The farmers' market was Gwen's home away from home.

"Thanks for doing this," I said after a minute.

"No problem. I figured you could use some cheering up."

I straightened slightly. "Why? I'm not—"

"Hey," he said gently. "It's okay."

I felt my body relax into the seat cushion. It *was* okay, I decided. After all, it was my sixteen-and-a-quarter birthday.

We got to Cape May around noon and walked along the chilly, mostly empty beach.

"What are you doing?" I asked Alex as he pulled a tiny plastic tube from the pocket of his jeans.

"Zinc oxide," he explained, squirting a strip of bright green lotion onto his palm. "UV rays are surprisingly strong on days like this. Want some?"

I shook my head as he spread the goo across his face. "You do know that stuff's green, right?"

Alex smiled. "Yeah, I grabbed it from Ginger's knapsack. Do I look like the Incredible Hulk?"

I giggled. "More like a string bean." I leaned over and plucked a small white shell out of the sand. "What's this one called?"

Alex glanced over. "*Crepidula fornicata*," he rattled off automatically. "Slipper shell."

I ran my thumb over the surface, feeling the bumps and ridges.

Alex bent down and picked up a fan-shaped disk. "*Chlamys nobilis*," he said.

"Now you're just showing off."

Smiling, Alex pulled his arm back and released. The shell whipped through the air and bounced through the surf before disappearing under the water.

I turned to him. "Cool. Show me how to do that."

"It's easy," he said, coming up behind me. He dropped a stone into my palm and lifted my arm gently, extending it against his.

I looked around. The beach was completely deserted. School, Kylie Frank, Tanner Mullins . . . out here, they were all so easy to forget. It was just Alex and me, alone with the sand and the waves.

If Alex were my boyfriend, this would be really romantic.

I jerked away from him. Where had *that* come from?

"What's wrong?" Alex asked, his forehead wrinkling.

I looked at him, at his bright green skin and smart brown eyes. It wasn't a perfect face. Far from it. His features weren't chiseled like Tanner Mullins's and his nose was definitely too long.

Then again, comparing any face to Tanner Mullins's was hardly fair. It was like doing a taste test between a filet mignon and a Big Mac.

Still, Alex definitely had a certain appeal. He was the sort of guy mothers were always saying nice things about, like, "That boy is gonna make some woman very happy one day."

Actually, my mom said that. All the time.

I looked down at Alex's hand, which was streaked with green grease. Long, wiry fingers fanned out from a wide, round palm. It was, I decided, a goofy-looking hand. Way too goofy for me. I wanted something smoother. More "leading man" than "funny sidekick."

For some reason, the thought made me feel better. I turned toward Alex and smiled.

"Nothing," I said, stepping forward. "Show me."

SEVEN

"**L**ooks like someone's having a party," Alex said as he eased the station wagon down my car-lined street.

Every light was on at Kylie's house. Crowds of people were visible through all the windows, and the bricks seemed to vibrate, pulsing with music and excitement.

I straightened. Of course. Tonight was Kylie's party. How could I have forgotten what was sure to be *the* Woodlawn social event of the year? I'd never managed to wrangle an invite, but thanks to homeroom and my here-but-not-here social status, I'd overheard dozens of party-planning tidbits. At this point, I could give a detailed account of what Kylie, Jules and Ella were wearing—wedge heels included—*and* recite the exclusive guest list by heart.

From the number of cars, though, the list couldn't have been all that exclusive.

It definitely excluded me, though.

I watched a couple of guys roll a keg across the Franks' lawn.

"I wonder if the cops will shut them down?" Alex mused. His tone was completely neutral, like he didn't care either way.

And he didn't. Alex didn't care about Kylie's party. He didn't care if the cops came, and he definitely didn't care that he hadn't been invited. That last thought would never even occur to him. Not in a million years. In just a few minutes, he'd pull out of my driveway and leave the whole scene behind, without even a backward glance.

He was lucky.

I tried to force myself to think about the day. We'd stayed at the beach until almost nine. Alex had taken me to dinner at a restaurant called the Mad Batter, where we'd stuffed ourselves with huge bowls of clam chowder, crab cakes the size of tennis balls and, because Alex had been sure to tell every patron and employee about my "special day," chocolate cake with a candle stuck in it. Much to my mortified delight, he even sang "Happy Birthday," his animated face glowing bright green above the flame.

It had been great.

Only now it was ruined. How could I enjoy anything when, in each and every single over-populated room in Kylie Frank's house, Wood-lawn history was being made?

And I wasn't even a tiny part of it.

Alex was talking, I realized suddenly. I hadn't heard a word, but his lips moved and now he was staring at me, waiting for some sort of response. Maybe a thank-you for the perfect day. Or a new joke about this being the best quarter birthday any girl could ever wish for.

I stared at him. At his still-green face and the too-long mop of black curls, the tips of which were now tinged with zinc oxide.

And that's when the anger hit—suddenly, in-explicably and almost painfully. It spread over me, poisoning the sweetness of our day.

Why?

Why was nothing the way I wanted it to be? Why had I never even come close to breaking my lame eleven o'clock curfew? Why were my friends quirky and offbeat instead of stylish and blond, with sleek cars and the right sort of clothing? Why didn't they *care* about sleek cars and the right sort of clothing?

Would it have *killed* Kylie Frank to invite me to her party? Of course, to do that she'd first have to acknowledge my existence, but given the fact that we shared a street and a homeroom, you'd *think* she'd figure it out.

It wasn't fair.

I turned my head away from Alex, back toward the party. Beside me, I felt him tense.

"Sam," he said softly. "Did you hear me?"

"Huh?" I asked. "Sorry. What did you say?"

Alex blinked. "Nothing. I just wished you a happy quarter birthday, that's all."

I'm a terrible person, I thought. *I'm sitting next to one of the best friends I'll ever have and all I can think about is trading up for an Abercrombie & Fitch model.*

"Thanks for today," I said. "It was perfect. Really."

Alex smiled as I pushed open the car door. "Talk to you tomorrow? Remember, you have a geometry test Monday."

I groaned. "Thanks for reminding me."

Alex shrugged. "Call if you need help."

I waved as he pulled out of the driveway. Turning slightly, I took a hesitant step toward Kylie's yard.

I could walk in. Just like that. So what if I

wasn't on the guest list. What could they do? Call clique control?

My eyes swept over the house, stopping on the second floor. Through the window I could see Tanner and Kylie standing together, his arm draped across her back. Jules stood on Kylie's other side, smiling adoringly.

They all looked so comfortable, which made sense. The party was their natural habitat.

For the first time that day, I considered—and instantly regretted—my outfit. It didn't help that I was also covered with sand and my hands and face were sticky from the cake.

I took an involuntary step backward. Then another. Before I knew it, I was in my house, heading for the safety of my bedroom. I could hear music playing in the distance, low and teasing.

I got into bed and shoved my head underneath the pillow with so much force I hit the bedpost. It hurt but I didn't care. I was still mad. Mad at Kylie Frank for not wanting to share even a little of herself with me. Mad at my parents for sticking me with socially inferior genes that guaranteed a lifetime of nights identical to this one. And mad at myself for being the sort of person A-listers didn't notice.

And for being the sort of person who cared. Deeply.

"I'm a terrible, shallow person," I said out loud to my empty room. I closed my eyes and fell asleep. And even though I really wanted to dream about the day at the beach, I'm pretty sure I didn't.

EIGHT

A keg of beer changed my life. I know that sounds weird—especially coming from someone who, until just a few months ago, had no idea how to operate one. (Okay. Forget operate. I'd never even seen a keg.) Not to mention the fact that I think all beer tastes like mucus. Still, I stand by the statement. A keg of beer changed my life. And in a pretty major way too.

When I woke up the next morning, the first thing I did was hop out of bed and look out my window. I had a great view of Kylie's house—the side as well as the front and back yards.

I'm not really sure what I was looking for. Traces of the party, I guess. But since I hadn't really been to a party since a Chuck E. Cheese sort of age, I had no idea what to expect.

At first glance, I was actually a little disappointed. Kylie Frank's house looked fine. Totally fine. The cars, people and music were all gone. The sun was up, so I couldn't tell if any of the lights were still on, but the lawn looked pretty pristine. No toilet paper-strewn shrubs or crushed beer cans in the grass or passed-out bodies lining the driveway. It was just a neat suburban house with a neat suburban lawn. If it had been warm outside, I'm sure I'd have heard birds chirping through the window.

And then I saw it. The keg Tanner and his friends had rolled into the house was now sitting in the middle of the front yard. It was sparkling, which at first I thought was because of the way the sun struck the metal surface. But when I squinted and looked a little closer, I realized the whole keg—and the area around it—was covered with glass.

Kylie Frank sat on the steps of her porch just a few feet away, talking on her cell. Her hands were fluttering around, and after a few seconds, she leapt to her feet and started pacing.

Something was happening. I pressed my ear

against the window, then drew back immediately. It was a stupid thing to do. Not only because the glass was freezing, but also because I wasn't bionic. As sharp as my eavesdropping skills were, I was too far away to hear anything.

Dressing quickly, I flew down the steps and out the front door, careful not to let it slam. Then I cut across the front yard and positioned myself behind the tree closest to Kylie. When I poked my head out, I saw what had her so upset.

The picture window on the first floor of her house was shattered. The remains were scattered everywhere—the grass, the keg, the porch. It was a mess.

"I can't believe it," Kylie was saying into the phone. She was still wearing her outfit from the night before—a gray trapeze dress with knee-high black patent leather boots. And even though her clothes looked slept-in and her hair was a little more rumpled than usual, she looked way better than I did despite my perfect bedtime hygiene and nine-plus hours of sleep.

"Seriously," she continued. "How drunk can you get? They threw a *keg* out my window." She paused as the person on the other end responded. "Okay, fine. The beer funnel was a bad idea. But Ella, my parents get home *tomorrow*. They're going to *kill* me."

I leaned forward a little, then stepped out

from behind the tree. I was gaping, but it wasn't like Kylie was even looking at me.

Yet.

"I *did* ask them to pay for it," Kylie snapped. "Nobody has any money." She frowned slightly, raking her hand through her hair. "I'm sorry. I know you're just trying to help. Listen, I'll call you back, okay? I need to think."

I watched as Kylie flipped her phone shut and buried her head in her hands. My pulse kicked up a notch as the realization hit. For the first time in my whole, completely lackluster high school career, I had something that Kylie Frank needed.

I ran back up to my bedroom and grabbed the pink metal cash box my grandmother had given to me when I was eight. At the time I'd used it for my various collections—candy, marbles, shells— but I'd cleaned it out when I'd started baby-sitting. At this point it was stuffed. Almost nine hundred dollars, not including the forty I'd made Friday night. I had no idea how much Kylie needed—I wasn't sure if she knew. Still, it was something.

As I walked downstairs and back outside, I racked my brain for a proverb about kegs and opportunity. The equivalent of "when one door closes another opens." The closest I got was "Ninety-Nine Bottles of Beer," which actually wasn't very close at all, but I didn't mind. All the events surrounding the keg disaster spread out before me like pages in a book. And I was pretty sure—no, I was positive—that I was in one of the chapters. At *least* one.

But when I reached Kylie, I hesitated. The usual anxiety triggered by close proximity to A-listers twisted my stomach. Money or no money, this was Kylie Frank. Sure, I'd sat behind her. I'd walked near her. I'd studied her from a safe distance and listened in on her conversations. But my one and only attempt to engage her in an actual conversation had crashed and burned. Completely.

I looked down at the cash box and winced. It reeked eighth birthday. Why hadn't I just shoved the money into my pocket?

Quit stalling, I ordered. *It's now or never.*

I opened my mouth. "Hey," I said.

Kylie looked up at me, her eyes narrowing slightly, like she was trying to place my face somewhere in her full, party-soaked life. Her expression reminded me of all the times I'd stood in front of my closet searching hopelessly for clothing I simply didn't own. Kylie Frank could think all day; she'd never find me.

It was painful to watch.

"I'm Sam," I said quickly. "Your neighbor. And I, uh, sit behind you in homeroom."

Kylie nodded distractedly, but I couldn't tell if her nod meant "Right. Of course that's you," or "Whatever. Let's just move on."

She waved toward the broken window. "Um, I'm sort of in the middle of a crisis here."

I took a deep breath. "Right. I mean, that's why I came over. I think maybe I can help." I flipped open the cash box and pushed it forward.

Kylie's gaze settled on the neat roll of bills, her blue eyes widening with surprise. "I don't get it," she said, after a minute. "You came over to give me all your money? Just like that?"

I shrugged. "Um, sort of. Well, maybe not all. But some. And I'm not *giving* it to you. It's more of a loan."

Kylie leaned back against the steps and stared up at me, cool and expectant.

"We could work out, like, a payment plan," I said, pushing out the words.

"A payment plan," Kylie repeated, her voice flat.

I cleared my throat. Why was this so hard? "Right. Weekly. Or, I don't know, monthly, if that works better for you."

She straightened slightly. "Why?" she asked. For the first time ever, she sounded genuinely interested in my answer.

I stared down at my feet. What could I say? *You're the most popular girl in school and by* lending you money I'm linking us together, forcing a "Kylie and Sam" situation? And any resulting attention you pay me is way more valuable than cash?

"I don't know. It's just—" I swallowed. "Why do you care? You need the money. I have money—"

"I don't know," Kylie said. "It just seems weird."

I looked at her. She was trying to sneer now, but something held her back.

Nerves, I realized with a rush. *Kylie Frank is nervous.*

Go on, whispered a little voice inside my head. *You're making progress. She needs you.*

I slapped the lid over the cash box and gave the combination dial a playful twist. "You're right," I said cheerfully. "Just forget it. Tell your parents I'm really sorry about the window. And let me know what homeschooling's like."

I spun around and headed back across the yard. I'd barely cleared the porch when Kylie's voice rang out.

"Wait!"

I turned as Kylie walked toward me.

That's right. Kylie Frank—*the* Kylie Frank—was following *me*.

"I'll take it," Kylie said, extending her hand. "Let me get the window fixed and we can work something out. That payment plan."

I hesitated. "You can't just take the money and ditch me," I warned. I took a deep breath. "I know about the party. I can always tell."

Kylie shot me a measuring sort of look, as if trying to decide something about me or the situation in general.

"I won't ditch you," she said finally. "I'll get you the money. I don't have a job or anything, but I'll figure it out."

Gingerly, I placed the cash box in her hand. "Deal," I said, relieved.

I watched as Kylie opened her front door and disappeared inside. She hadn't bothered to thank me, but I decided not to let that bother me.

I was at my front door when I remembered the cash box's lock. Kylie would need the combination if she ever wanted to spend the money. Turning around, I walked back to Kylie's house and rang the bell. I could hear music playing— something loud and poppy I'm sure every high schooler in the country would recognize except me.

"Hello?" I called out, rapping my hand against the door. It swung open and I stepped inside.

Kylie's house had the exact same layout as mine. It was trashed from the party the night before.

Still, it looked a lot cooler.

Where my house was filled with lots of old, overstuffed furniture, purchased by my parents from local flea markets and thrift stores for their "history and character," everything in Kylie's house was sleek and modern. Couches were flat and boxy. Trinkets didn't exist. And they had a plasma-screen TV. Several, in fact. My parents wouldn't even get cable. ("Why bother?" my mother always asked every time I suggested it. "We get PBS.")

"Kylie?" Following the music, I headed up the stairs and walked down the hall toward an open door.

The room was empty, but the television and stereo were both on and I could hear water running. Standing in the doorway, I studied the room, absorbing the pale blue walls covered with friendship collages and framed pictures. There was Kylie in her pep squad uniform, making poly-blend look sexy. There she was again, just the perfect amount of soaked, washing cars for Unicef with the rest of the A-listers. It was all there, right in front of me: homecoming queen, Spring Fling, fall fashion show . . . the high school life that existed for everyone but me.

I turned away from the pictures and then really wished I hadn't.

Kylie Frank was standing in front of me, completely naked.

Being flashed by the most popular girl in school was definitely not how I'd pictured the morning. (But okay, while we're on the subject and because I'm sure you're wondering, naked Kylie Frank was, if possible, even more sickeningly perfect than the fully clothed version. Flat-stomach-long-legs-make-you-want-to-hit-the-gym-and-then-kill-yourself perfect.) Besides that, I'm not really a nude sort of person. I don't even like being naked when I'm supposed to be naked—like in dressing rooms or before I take a shower. Usually, I carry my clothes into the bathroom with me so that I can hop back into them as soon as possible.

So sure, the au naturel factor was definitely disconcerting. But there was something else going on too.

Something far more disturbing.

Kylie lifted her arms up behind her neck and unzipped her skin.

NINE

She didn't see me, at least not at first. I just stood there, gaping, as Kylie pulled the zipper down her back and wriggled. As she moved, I actually saw something—something flesh-colored—slip down the perfect column of her body.

The material started to shimmer. The looser it got, the more it sparkled. What had moments before spread over Kylie's body and disappeared like a second skin now looked more like a nude-colored catsuit. Or a body stocking dusted with glitter.

Was it a girdle? But I was pretty sure nobody but my grandma Frieda even wore girdles anymore.

Especially not Kylie Frank, the most perfectly proportioned girl in the tristate area. She had no use for lipo-lingerie or undercover body shaping. She didn't even need control-top panty hose.

Or did she? I narrowed my eyes slightly as Kylie stepped completely out of the suit. She still looked good: flat stomach, toned limbs and not a ripple or pucker in sight. But her skin had lost its tawny, sun-kissed glow. It looked pastier, like the pale, dry midwinter skin everyone on the East Coast—myself included—suffered through.

Whatever it was she'd been wearing was better than spring break and a tanning bed combined.

"What *is* that?" I blurted out.

Startled, Kylie turned her head, met my gaze and screamed.

"What are you doing here?" she shrieked. The suit was now completely off, and it rested in her hands, limp and twinkling. When she saw me looking at it, she shoved it behind her back and out of sight.

I wiped my suddenly clammy hands on my jeans. Even though Kylie was the naked one, there was something in her tone that made me feel vulnerable.

"I'm sorry," I apologized. "I—I just wanted to give you the combination to the cash box—"

"I can't believe you just barged in here!" she cried, cutting me off. "Who does that? Get out!"

She was panicked. I could see it in her face. Her eyes were wide and jumpy and her cheeks were drawn. It was weird to see her like this, so anxious and, well, scared.

But it also gave me strength. Because I knew, right then and there, that there was more to Kylie's mystery undergarment than seamless support and an invisible panty line. And—call it insight born from years of frustrated popularity fantasies—I also knew that it was somehow tied to my social success.

"What were you wearing before?" I demanded, trying desperately to keep my eyes focused on her face. I'd never actually had a conversation with a completely naked person, and it was very disconcerting. Not to mention icky. "You have to tell me."

Kylie shook her head. "If you don't get out right now, I'll call the cops."

I squared my shoulders. "Good idea. Maybe they'll fix your window and roll the keg off the lawn."

Her eyes flashed. "I mean it! Leave!"

I crossed my arms over my chest and forced what I hoped was a don't-mess-with-me look onto my face. "Not until you explain."

"I'm not explaining anything to you," Kylie said with a sneer.

"Well, unless you want to blowtorch the cash box," I said, surprising myself, "it seems like you don't have a choice." I was tempted to toss in a "tough noogies" for good measure but decided to quit while I was ahead.

"God, you're pathetic," Kylie spit, but a muscle under her eye had started to twitch and I could see that I'd gotten to her.

"Tell me," I said. "Or bye-bye bay window."

"Look, I can't," she sputtered. Her hands were still behind her back and she stood rigid, as if she were afraid to move. "I'm not supposed to . . . you don't understand."

"I understand that money is often exchanged for goods and services," I pointed out.

Kylie sighed. Her shoulders drooped a little as she slowly pulled the catsuit out from behind her back.

I stepped closer for a better look. As I moved, the suit winked at me.

"Uh, that's not Victoria's Secret, is it?" I guessed. "I mean, what *is* that?"

Kylie stared down at the Skin with a wistful, almost reverent expression on her face. "This," she whispered, "is popular."

A ripple of anxiety shot down my spine.

Yikes. Major yikes. Clearly, Kylie Frank was insane. Possibly even dangerous.

"Look, why don't you keep the money?" I reasoned, thinking that my chances of becoming popular would be even more diminished if I was chopped up and living in Kylie's freezer. "It's okay. I'll just go now and you can, um, find your clothes and call Home Depot. The combination's really easy—two-four-six-eight—but I can write it down if you—"

"What, you don't believe me?" Kylie said, sauntering across the carpet toward her dresser. My discomfort seemed to have restored her confidence. "Well, it's true."

"What's true?" I asked.

"The Skin," Kylie said as she opened the bottom drawer and tucked the suit neatly inside. She pulled out a T-shirt and slipped it on over her head.

I was so relieved she wasn't naked anymore I actually felt a little faint.

"The Skin?" I asked.

"You should be happy, you know," Kylie continued, plucking a pair of bikini undies from the drawer. "Everyone thinks popularity is a *quality*—like thick hair or a great sense of humor—when really it has nothing to do with any of that."

I stared at her. "It doesn't," I repeated, but the way it came out, it sounded more like a question.

Kylie shook her head. "Nope." She waved a hand toward the dresser. "It's all about the Skin."

"I don't get it," I said, shaking my head for what felt like the hundredth time. "You're saying that that *thing* is why you're so popular? How?"

Kylie flashed me a smile. "You know, I have absolutely no idea. I got it the night before freshman year—it was just sitting under my pillow along with a user's manual and a set of rules. I've been wearing it ever since."

I stared at her, waiting for a big laugh and a loud "*Kidding!*"

When neither came, I finally spoke.

"And you didn't find this just a little strange?"

Kylie swiped a pair of terry-cloth sweatpants off her floor and pulled them on. "Well, sure. I mean, I almost threw the whole thing out." She reached up and swept her long blond hair into a high ponytail. "But then I read the rules and it . . ." She trailed off as if trying to remember. "I guess it just seemed too good to pass up. The note said there was one in every school, so I figured, why not?" She shrugged. "You know what I mean."

"Okay," I said, gathering my thoughts together. "You're saying that these *skins* are, like, everywhere?"

Kylie frowned. "No. Like I said, there's one per school. You know how every school has an It-girl? Well, every It-girl has a Skin."

"And that's what makes them It-girls? Isn't that a little *Invasion of the Body Snatchers*?"

Kylie snorted. "Hardly. I mean, this isn't a mind-control sort of thing. I'm still the same person, with or without the Skin. I guess it's just sort of . . ." She frowned, searching for the right word. "I don't know. Magic?"

I stared at her, not sure what to say.

"Listen, you can't tell anyone about this," Kylie warned. "I'm serious."

"I won't," I muttered. "It's too crazy for gossip."

Kylie laughed. "This from the girl willing to fork over her entire life savings just to sit at the cool table." She shot me a look. "It's not that crazy."

TEN

"Is this too bitter?"

I snapped my head up and looked at Gwen. We were sitting in her kitchen, surrounded by cookbooks and various pots and pans. Her arm was extended, holding out a mixing bowl filled with some sort of bright yellow jelly.

I peered inside. "Mmm . . . looks good. Can I taste?"

Gwen rolled her eyes. "Thanks for tuning in. I've only been asking you for the past five minutes."

I swept my finger around the rim of the bowl and into my mouth. "Yum," I said. "Lemon?"

"Persimmon," she corrected. "I told you that, too. Seriously, Sam, what's with you?" She glanced down at the yellow mix and frowned. "If it tastes like lemon, I added too much zest."

"It tastes great," I assured her. "Really."

"I'm not sure I can trust you," Gwen said, shaking her head. "What with your recent lobotomy and all."

"What lobotomy?" Alex asked, strolling into the room. He was carrying Gwen's Cuisinart in one hand and a pair of pliers in the other. "I think I fixed it," he told her, placing the machine on the counter. "But you have to quit overstuffing it. That's why it jams."

"Thanks," Gwen said as she poured an entire tray of ginger snaps down the Cuisinart's neck, ignoring Alex's glare. She nodded toward me. "I was just telling Sam she's been a serious space case lately."

I raised a hand in protest. "Please. I prefer the word *preoccupied*."

"I don't know," Alex said slowly. He pulled out a stool and sat down at the counter. "*Preoccupied* sounds a little intellectual. Like you're trying to stop global warming or something."

"Hey!" I said. "How do you know I haven't been?"

Gwen and Alex shared a look, then burst out laughing.

Alex glanced at my backpack and the magazine poking out of the front. " 'Why Celebs Don't Wear Underwear,' " he read from the cover. " 'What Flavor Lip Gloss Are You?' " He grinned, admiring the mustache and chest hair I'd doodled on a beaming rock diva. "Hey, can I borrow that after you're done?"

I scowled. "Fine. So I've been a little out of it. Big deal."

He cleared his throat and straightened. "So, uh, how was geometry? I never heard from you this weekend."

I squinted my eyes, trying to remember the test I'd taken only the day before. There had been shapes, definitely. And numbers. None of it had made any sense, but I'd somehow managed to plow through, handing in the papers without thinking of their inevitable return to me: marked up with angry red slashes and a bright red "See me" at the top.

That was what happened when I attempted math without Alex.

"It was fine," I muttered. "I haven't gotten it back yet."

Alex pursed his lips. "Seriously, Sam, what's going on?" he asked, his voice quiet.

I looked back and forth between my friends. Three days had passed since I'd found out about the Skin and I still hadn't said a word. I felt guilty too. It was huge news, and in the past I'd always shared huge news with them. Sure, Kylie Frank had sworn me to secrecy, but that wasn't what was keeping my mouth shut. I knew I could trust Gwen and Alex if I told them.

The truth was: I didn't want to tell them. I'd been trying, semisuccessfully, to convince myself that this was their fault. *They* were the ones with the ultranegative attitudes, the ones who mocked everything high school. So what, I reasoned, made the Skin any different?

They probably wouldn't even care, I kept repeating. *They think popularity's stupid, so why bother?*

Given what I'd just learned, I guess they kind of had a point. After all my coveting and craving, being popular wasn't such a riddle after all. It wasn't reserved for thin-limbed girls named Ashley. And more importantly, it wasn't some sort of indecipherable code specifically designed to keep people like me, with subpar hair and fashion-challenged wardrobes, out. *Teen Vogue* had been right all along. Popularity wasn't about who you were.

It was about what you wore.

I wish I could say that the realization was liberating, that the secret helped me get over the whole thing. I wish it helped me stop caring.

But knowing that popularity was as simple as

slipping on a pair of Spanx (and, from the looks of things, a lot less binding) had actually made things worse. I was more obsessed than ever. Because the more I thought about it—and over the past few days it had been the only thing I thought about—the more I wondered: if popularity was so easy, then why couldn't I have it? Why not me?

All I needed was the Skin.

Sadly, that was the only thought that felt truly liberating. I'd spent all of high school so far wishing I could trade up. Myself, my hair, my clothes. I'd wasted so much time and energy trying to become a better version of myself. I'd memorized every "How to Be Popular" article published in the last decade, to the point where I could recite not only the contents but also the author and date of publication. I'd suffered through so many painful and just plain stupid self-improvement ploys—from lazy push-up bras that refused to push up anything to body sugaring. (Don't ask. Just don't do it.) And all because I thought *I* was to blame for the total nonevent that was my high school career.

Well, now I knew. My lack of polish and social grace had absolutely nothing to do with anything. Popularity wasn't personal. The only thing keeping me from the top of the spirit pyramid was a thing. A piece of *hosiery*.

And I wanted it. Desperately.

This was the real reason I kept the Skin to myself. If I said as much to Alex and Gwen, they'd only argue with me. They'd be completely disgusted, if they even believed me. And they'd definitely try to talk me out of what I was certain would be my next move.

I was going to steal the Skin.

It was an awful thing to think—and do—but really, the more I thought about it the more sense it made. Besides, what choice did I have? Kylie Frank had been wearing the Skin for almost two years. She'd used my hard-earned money to fix her window and, crisis averted, had plunged seamlessly back into her fab life. Wasn't there something wrong with that? Wasn't it time for her to share?

I squeezed my eyes closed and tried to shut out all the ugliness.

"Sam," Alex said. I opened one eye and looked at him. "Are you sure you're okay?"

"Oh my god. The persimmons. Do you think you have food poisoning?" Gwen gasped and spun around. "I think we have some Pepto in the bathroom."

"No, no," I said, laughing in spite of myself. "I'm fine. I swear. I just . . ." I looked at Alex and said the first thing that popped into my head. "The test was a disaster. I shouldn't be allowed to open a geometry book without you around to chaperone."

Alex smiled easily and placed his hand lightly on my shoulder. "Is that what's bothering you? Forget it. We'll crush them on the next one."

Gwen bent down and pulled open the oven door. The room immediately filled with comforting, familiar Gwen-scents: Cinnamon. Melted butter. Vanilla.

"Here," she said, deftly extracting a sheet of brightly covered pastries. "Persimmon squares make everything better."

"Plus," Alex told me, "they're squares. So technically, you're studying."

"Thanks," I said, leaning toward the sheet and pointedly ignoring the little twang in my chest.

ELEVEN

It's possible to justify anything. Because, really, aren't there at least two sides to every situation? Isn't that what's so wrong with the paparazzi's relentless persecution of celebrities?

This is what I told myself as I snuck across the Franks' yard and swiped the spare key from underneath the flowerpot, like I'd seen Kylie do a hundred times before.

This isn't *evil*, I reasoned as I slid the key into the lock. *It's active. Proactive.* I was trying to turn my life around. I was evening the social scale . . . and if I happened to tip the balance a little in my favor, well, I was only human.

I let myself into Kylie's house and climbed the stairs. I'd been stressing about the whole breaking-and-entering thing for almost a week but it turned out to be a lot easier than I'd expected. So easy, in fact, I wondered why my whole street wasn't robbed more often. Like on a daily basis.

Even though I was sure no one was home, I tiptoed all the way to Kylie's bedroom, just to be sure. I brushed aside the DO NOT DISTURB sign that hung from the doorknob, noting with satisfaction that it had been swiped from a Marriott.

See, I thought as I cut across the room and opened the closet door. *I'm not the only thief.*

I stood there for a minute, absorbing the colorful terrain that was Kylie Frank's wardrobe. There were tiny pleated skirts and satin skinny pants, plus about a dozen pairs of jeans. The whole spread looked like an "after" snapshot from a *Seventeen* closet makeover. I could just picture the article in my head: "Go from Forgettable to Fashionista with Just a Few of These Must-Haves!"

Shoving aside the hangers, I tucked myself in between a navy coat and a bright red wrap dress.

And then I waited.

It was actually really boring. I mean, in the movies, break-ins are always these heart-pounding, nail-biting affairs, filled with *Mission:*

Impossible-style music, Brad Pitt look-alikes and leggy, leather-clad brunettes. But here I was, sitting at the bottom of someone else's closet (sure, it was one of the more fashionable closets I'd seen, but it was still a closet) trying desperately not to nod off.

The scene was hardly movieworthy. It was barely even soap opera material.

I was braiding my hair for the tenth time when, finally, the energy in the room seemed to shift. There were footsteps in the hall and then the door swung open.

"I'm so sorry!" Kylie Frank was saying as she breezed in. I could hear her footsteps on the carpet, then a thud as she dropped something—a bag, maybe—onto the floor. "I wanted to meet you, but Tanner had a game. He gets really upset when I don't watch him play. Then he wanted to work out afterwards, so I got stuck at the gym. . . ."

I peeked through a crack in the door. Kylie stood over her bed, iPhone at her ear. "I know, I know. You should definitely hate me. It's just I'm *so* busy all the time. I really have to get a grip." She paused for a response, then sighed. "I swear, we'll hit the mall tomorrow, okay, Ellie? Listen, I gotta go. I'm all sweaty and I've got, like, a million hours of homework. See ya."

Kylie pressed a few buttons on her phone, then tossed it onto the bed. I watched anxiously as she unpacked her leather hobo bag (three notebooks, a sweater and a makeup case the size of a Honda).

"You have sixteen new messages," chirped the voice-mail woman.

Whoa. Sixteen? How was that even possible? We'd only been out of school for, what, three hours?

"Hey Kylie, it's Matt. Just calling to say hi. Hope the move went well . . ."

Matt Kane. The guy Kylie had dumped for Tanner. I thought back to that other morning in homeroom. What had Ella said? *Matt really likes you. . . .*

Based on his tone, I had to agree. I barely knew Matt—and I was sure he wouldn't know me if I fell on him—but I couldn't help feeling a little sorry for the guy. It was obvious he was trying to leave one of those light-and-breezy sort of messages. But what was even more obvious was that he was completely head-over-heels for Kylie Frank. His voice was a dead giveaway.

Kylie reached for the phone, snapping it shut with a groan. When she turned around, her expression caught me off guard.

She looked sad, not annoyed.

Scooping her bag off the floor, she fished out a framed picture. I couldn't make out what it was, but it seemed to cheer her up.

"I'm just feeling sorry for Matt," Kylie said to the picture as she placed it gently on her nightstand. "But that's stupid. Matt sounded fine. Great."

Are you hearing-impaired? I felt like asking. *The guy actually sounds like a lovesick puppy.*

There was a knock on the door, and then Mrs. Frank poked her head into the room. Her platinum hair was twisted into a knot and she wore a tan suit with chocolate suede pumps, just the sort of outfit I'd imagined she owned during our first meeting.

"Hey," Kylie said, turning to face her mother.

Mrs. Frank's gaze slid from the pile of notebooks scattered across the floor to a neat column of boxes stacked in a corner of the room.

"I'm about to start dinner," she said. Her voice was clipped and reminded me of when she'd mistaken me for one of Kylie's friends. "Have you finished your homework?"

"Not yet. I'm working on it."

Mrs. Frank frowned. "Those boxes aren't going to just pop open and unpack themselves, Kylie."

"I *know.*" A slight edge had crept into Kylie's voice.

"Well, we've been here for a month. Your father and I are almost done with every other room in the house," her mother said as her eyes zeroed in on Kylie's cell phone. She sighed. "Please don't tell me you've been on the phone this whole time."

"I *wasn't.*"

Mrs. Frank turned and placed her hand on the doorknob. "I'm heading back downstairs. I thought I'd just make some pasta and a salad."

"Sure," Kylie said. I could tell she was relieved. She'd definitely gotten off easy.

"Please don't make me take away your phone," her mother said quietly.

She closed the door behind her and I watched as Kylie sank back down onto the bed.

So, I thought. *There are certain things the Skin can't protect you from. Like parents.*

Was Kylie wishing, like I had so many times, that she had a different sort of mother? A mom you could take shopping without fear of public humiliation? The sort of mom who offered advice without judgment and enjoyed the occasional ice cream pig-out slash heart-to-heart?

Maybe Kylie Frank and I shared something else in common besides nine hundred dollars and the secret to popularity.

Kylie walked across the room through an arched doorway I assumed led to her bathroom. A few seconds later, I heard the sound of water running and Kylie returned, stripping off her clothes.

There was the Skin—smooth and perfect. I watched as she reached behind her neck and unzipped, then peeled the whole thing off. It hung limply in her hands as she stepped across the room, opened the bottom drawer of her dresser and tucked it neatly inside.

My heart pounded as Kylie stepped back inside the bathroom and shut the door.

It was now or never.

There was only one small problem. Okay, two: my legs had stopped working, *and* I was on the verge of hyperventilating.

I took a deep breath. *I've never stolen anything in my life*, I thought. *And, really, what has Kylie Frank ever done to me?*

I remembered Kylie's face as her mother was lecturing her. She'd looked small, somehow. Not nearly as poised. Or perfect.

I pushed myself onto my feet. I couldn't do it. It just wasn't going to happen.

I walked across Kylie's room, fully committed to my decision.

I was halfway to the door when it hit me. Full force.

Popularity was everywhere: on the friendship collages that wallpapered Kylie's bedroom; the twelve new e-mails that had just popped up on Kylie's iBook; and in the framed picture on Kylie's nightstand . . . of Kylie kissing Tanner Mullins.

Kylie was *kissing* Tanner Mullins.

I stared at the picture. It was a great shot. Tanner leaned into Kylie, their faces flushed with excitement. Kylie's head tilted off to one side, playful in a sexy, kitten-heels sort of way.

They looked so perfect. So romantic. So very, very high school . . .

I turned my back on the picture and retraced my steps across the room.

Slowly, deliberately, I opened the chest and grabbed the Skin.

I held my breath and tiptoed out of the room. A door was open at the end of the hall and I could hear the murmur of voices. Kylie's parents, I guessed.

I stepped carefully down the stairs, trying to avoid any attention-grabbing creaks, and shot out the front door.

And then I ran.

TWELVE

Cheap nylons.

If you're wondering what it feels like to hold popularity in your hands, head directly to the hosiery aisle at your nearest Target and rip open a carton of nylons. Avoid name brands; they're way too high-end. Popularity is more Hanes than Donna Karan. It's totally synthetic, without a touch of silk.

And it was mine. All mine.

When I got back to my room, I shut my door and spread the Skin out on my bed.

"What happens now?" I asked, half expecting the thing to answer me.

But it just sat there, lifeless and shriveled, like a flesh-colored union suit. It reminded me of this special I once saw on Oxygen: *Body Image, Exposed.* All these women of various weights and shapes wore nude body stockings, then stood in front of a mirror and explained how they felt ("My reflection really makes me regret all those Whoppers"). It was actually pretty interesting, especially when one of the women—a tall, über-leggy blonde—fell so in love with her pseudo-naked self that she wore the body stocking to her local grocery store and got arrested.

I stared at the Skin. If I put it on, what would my reflection tell me? Would my life instantly change? And how about my appearance? Kylie had looked pretty much the same in and out of the Skin, but maybe I was different. Anything seemed possible.

Really, I wondered. *What now?*

You're a thief. It doesn't belong to you. Give it back.

The words popped into my head before I could stop them.

It was true. I'd stolen popularity.

My heart thumped inside my chest.

It wasn't too late to return it. Sure, I'd have to sneak back into the Franks' house, which was definitely pressing my luck. But Kylie was probably still in the shower. If I left now—right now—I could tuck the Skin back inside the drawer and then slip out. No one would know what I'd almost done.

And nothing would change. That was a definite. I'd be stuck with myself—not the new-and-improved version the Skin promised. I'd live out the rest of high school craving everything popular—and getting Gwen's brownies and computer Scrabble with Alex instead.

"I can't return popularity," I whined aloud, sounding exactly like a four-year-old at Toys "R" Us. "Who does that?"

I glanced down at my shoes—white canvas Keds. That said it all. *I* was a pair of Keds—colorless, plain and almost painfully flat.

Kylie Frank, on the other hand, was a stiletto.

Time for a shoe swap.

I went over to my desk, shut down my computer and turned off my phone. I was pretty sure Kylie had no idea what my e-mail or IM address was, but I wasn't taking any chances. The fewer ways to track me down, the better.

I walked back to the bed and picked up the Skin. And that was when I remembered the rules. Kylie had mentioned something about a set of rules. And a user's manual.

I had neither.

Okay, so I hadn't thought the plan completely through.

No biggie, I told myself. *You're smart. You can figure this out. It'll be like on-the-job training.*

When I'd first found out about the Skin, Kylie was removing it. And this afternoon she'd taken it off again to shower. So clearly, you didn't have to wear the Skin all the time.

I was making progress already.

But then there was the whole maintenance issue. I had no idea how to wrap my head around that one. I mean, I had the Skin, great. But how was I supposed to wash it? This wasn't the sort of thing you could research on Wikipedia—or by reading a box of Tide. Actually, forget Tide. Maybe I needed special soap. Or was the Skin dry clean only?

Yikes. What if I accidentally washed the popularity right out?

Maybe it was best to avoid washing altogether, even though Kylie Frank had worn the Skin less than a half hour ago. Or was that completely unsanitary, like buying used underwear or something? *Gross.* What if I got some sort of disease? Kylie seemed really healthy, but you never knew.

I held the Skin up to the light. It looked perfectly clean and smelled like, well, nothing at all. Maybe popularity was impervious to stains and odors.

Since that last thought was the only one that relaxed me, I decided to stick with it.

Quit stalling. If you want to be popular, you have to wear popular.

My stomach twisted as I heaved all the lingering questions out of my head and, before I could change my mind, stripped off all my clothes. I lifted the Skin, running my hands up and down the torso, looking for the zipper.

It was there, in the back. I pulled it down and stepped inside: first one leg, then the other, and finally my arms. I thought I'd have to tug a little—like an actual pair of nylons—but I didn't have to do any work at all. In a matter of seconds, the Skin spilled over me with a gentle *swoosh*, covering my body from neck to toe.

I was inside popularity. And it felt . . . great.

I edged the zipper up to my neck and looked down. I could still feel the Skin but I couldn't see it anymore. Anywhere. Including my feet (this struck me as particularly odd since, off the body, the Skin's feet weren't divided into toe compartments . . . but now my toes were totally free and completely wiggleable). As soon as I'd put it on, it had disappeared, melting over me, sleek and luxurious, like a really expensive body lotion.

And there was something else too. Maybe it was because the Skin felt so good. Or it could've been the magic working. Or maybe it had nothing to do with the Skin and was all in my head.

To this day, I still don't know, and at that particular moment I really didn't care. At all. Because the thing is, I felt amazing. Inside *and* out. Wearing the Skin, I was sure I stood taller. And my skin looked just a little creamier—smoother and slightly tanned.

I was *definitely* more leggy blond than Whopper woman.

Kylie's going to kill me, I thought, suddenly and with absolute certitude. No way was she going to let something like this slip out of her grasp without a fight. Nobody would.

I was safe for now, but I was definitely in for some ugliness—sooner rather than later.

Relax, said a voice inside my head—obviously not the same one that had just called me a thief. *Enjoy the moment.*

Great advice, I decided. Pulling on my pajamas, I strutted around the bedroom like a Victoria's Secret model decked out in this season's newest nightie (if this season's nightie happened to be a flannel gown from L.L. Bean . . . but whatever). I was bold. I was confident. I was completely un-me.

I glanced at my window and froze mid-sashay. The blinds were down but even so, I could easily guess what was going on next door. It wasn't hard to picture Kylie Frank, fresh from the shower, her towel-clad form bending over the empty bottom drawer. She'd check once, twice—maybe even a third and fourth time before diving into a panicked, desperate search for the Skin that would start in her bedroom and spread to other parts of the house. I was pretty sure she'd be up all night.

A twinge of anxiety worked its way down my spine.

So much for relaxing, I thought.

I couldn't help it. I was scared.

Plus, I felt guilty. I hated what I'd done, that my actions had cost someone else. It was collateral damage, sure, but it was awful. And it was all my fault.

On the other hand, my life was on the verge of a major rewrite. I was sure of it.

Popularity loved me. I couldn't just turn it away.

The phone rang in the hallway and my new, semiflattened stomach dropped somewhere below my knees.

Had Kylie Frank figured it out already? I was so dead.

"Sam, Alex!" my mother called from downstairs.

Relieved, I opened my door and cat-walked into the hall. "Hey," I said, scooping up the phone. There was the trace of a giggle in my voice.

"What's so funny?" Alex asked, amused.

"Nothing," I said. I carried the receiver back to my room and got into bed. The butterflies in my stomach swooped into my throat, making my voice jumpy and excited. "What's up?"

"Your cell was off, but I just thought I'd check in. You know, in case you had any questions."

"Tons," I said, smiling into the phone. "For starters, why do people always grab a million more napkins than they'll ever use from those dispensers in the cafeteria?"

Alex laughed. "I meant about geometry. The napkin thing is way out of my league."

"Don't sell yourself short," I told him. I yawned. "Listen, if you're *really* nice to me tomorrow, I'll let you check my work. Deal?"

"Wow, you're the best," Alex said gravely.

"I know. I'll see you tomorrow."

"Definitely."

I pushed the Off button and dropped the phone onto the floor next to my bed. It was a drain on the batteries and pretty much guaranteed a lecture from one or both parents on waste, but I didn't care.

I had the Skin. I had everything.

THIRTEEN

A new life, I decided the next morning, definitely deserved a new wardrobe.

I stood in front of my open closet, searching the depressing landscape for a Skinworthy outfit. I'd woken up early, strangely refreshed and surprised I'd been able to sleep at all considering that today was *the* day. Sam Klein was being relaunched into society, new and improved. And she had the power of the Skin behind her.

I was ready. More than ready.

Unfortunately, my wardrobe, having stalled somewhere around 2007, wasn't. Not by several seasons.

I flipped through the hangers, eyeing and dismissing each item in a matter of seconds. There were jean overalls (No thank you, Old McDonald), a brown burlap smock dress I was certain had been designed by Mr. Potato Head and green wide-wale cords that were perfect for Earth Day.

It's not like I expected to wake up to a whole new life, with a truckload of admirers, a brand-new Lexus and a closet filled with expensive bags and shoes. (Okay, that's exactly what I expected.)

But it wasn't my fault, I reasoned. How was I supposed to know how the Skin worked? I didn't have the manual or the rules.

This was definitely going to be a problem. Since I had no idea what sort of time restrictions, if any, applied to removing the Skin, I'd decided to sleep in it. This morning I'd taken it off to shower, since I'd seen Kylie do the same. I'd tucked it into a pink shoe box and, just to be safe, slid it under my bed. Postshower, it had slipped back on, smooth as silk. But I still had so many questions about its wear and use . . . and no place to go for answers.

All the It-girls have them, I heard Kylie saying. *One in every school.*

I straightened. If that was the case, then the world was filled with secret-Skin-wearing homecoming queens. Maybe there was some sort of network I could tap into. A support group for the magically popular? Or even better—a chat room.

I walked over to my computer and turned it on, carefully avoiding e-mail and IM. I googled the words *second skin* and sat back, waiting to be connected with A-listers around the world.

The results were a little disappointing. Second Skin was a blister treatment, a lab in Northern California, a gay bar in Chelsea and a foreign film that looked mildly pornographic. But not, according to my laptop, a magical wet suit.

Slightly frustrated, I got up and plucked the most neutral items I could find from the closet—black jeans and a long-sleeved gray T-shirt. They'd have to do. Besides, I was already wearing the *most* important item of all.

I checked my watch. It was only seven a.m. I was more than an hour early, which was perfect. I had to be out of the house by the time Kylie Frank woke up and pounded on my door. I shot off a quick IM to Gwen (Don't pik me up. G2G early 4 geo.), grabbed my knapsack and headed downstairs.

My parents were at the kitchen table, drinking coffee and reading the paper.

Both wielded scissors. This was their morning routine—massacring the newspaper and saving relevant articles for their various issues-related scrapbooks. The angry-looking albums filled our shelves—an alphabet of activism, from "Animal Rights!" to "Toxics!" peppered by the occasional organic cookbook.

Why, I wondered for the millionth time, *can't my parents just read mysteries and romances like normal adults?* If I ever found a Harlequin anywhere in my house, I'd seriously have it framed.

"You're up early," my mother chirped. She looked at me, her eyes widening slightly. "Are you wearing makeup?"

My heartbeat kicked up a notch. "No," I said, swiping a hand across my cheeks as if to prove my blush-free status. "Why?"

"I don't know," she mused, still studying me. "You just look . . . different." She rose from the table, placing her hands on her hips. "It's fine if you want to experiment with a little makeup, Sam, but please use a brand that doesn't animal-test. I can get you a list if you want."

"And don't buy anything from Walmart," my father added as his scissors moved swiftly across his paper. "Talk about union busting."

"Okeydoke," I said happily. Instead of being annoyed—my normal response to my parents' PC inquisitions—I actually felt hopeful. If my mom had noticed the difference, I hadn't imagined it:

the Skin was working. "But I don't really wear makeup."

My mother sighed loudly. "Just keep animal testing in mind. What goes on in those labs is criminal." She gave her head an angry shake. "Now, how about some oatmeal before you go?"

"I don't eat breakfast," I informed her. Again.

"Suit yourself." She shrugged, looking like I'd just told her I was dropping out of school to join a Kiss cover band. "It's only the most important meal of the day."

I glanced at my watch. "Fine," I muttered. We went through this every morning. "I guess I have time."

One bowl of organic mush later and I was on my way. I was halfway out the door when my father came rushing after me.

"Almost forgot these!" He handed me a stack of flyers. "I can't believe it's January already."

Every month, my father's law firm printed up a new flyer exposing the latest corporate criminal. Even though I'd never volunteered for the job, he'd appointed me "head of youth marketing," which basically meant I was supposed to post the flyers around school.

I usually stuck a few in the girls' room and ditched the rest.

It seemed that this month's evil empire was Nike, which, according to the flyer, abused workers in third-world nations. I studied the papers in my hand, absorbing the angry red swoosh and the warning: JUST DON'T DO IT.

"Isn't that sort of old news?" I asked.

My dad shrugged. "If it's still happening, it's not old."

I tucked the flyers under my arms and headed out. Kylie's house, I noted with more than a little relief, was completely dark and silent.

I speed-walked the six blocks to school, rushed through the heavy blue doors and dumped my things, including my dad's flyers, in my locker. Then I headed to the closest bathroom and locked myself in the first stall. I'd decided last night that, in order to avoid any early-morning run-ins, it was best to avoid homeroom completely.

I grabbed a magazine from my backpack and tried to read an article about celebrity cellulite but couldn't really focus. Instead, I doodled across the cover (if you ask me, every actress looks better with a goatee) as thoughts popped into my head like champagne corks.

The confidence from this morning was gone, replaced with nervous energy and a trace of doubt. In my room, anything had seemed possible, but at Woodlawn "anything" seemed a lot less likely.

Schools were supposed to be supportive and nurturing environments—at least according to the posters in the guidance counselor's office. But for me, Woodlawn had always had the opposite effect. Walking through the halls, I felt hopelessly unimportant, in danger of fading away completely.

I shifted uncomfortably, realizing that, at that very instant, I had a far more pressing problem than the stolen Skin or even Kylie Frank's wrath.

I had to pee.

The good news: I was in the bathroom, actually sitting on the toilet. The bad news: I was in the Skin. And, so far as I could tell, the only zipper ran vertically along my spine, not horizontally, um, a little farther downtown.

I had no choice. I'd have to take it off. All of it.

As quietly as I could, I slipped off my clothes, then worked the zipper down my spine, pulled my arms out of the Skin and gently tugged.

It's not that big a deal, I reasoned postflush. *Scuba divers must do this all the time.* Besides, if the Skin actually worked, it would definitely be worth the hassle.

The bell rang just as I was getting dressed. I

shoved the magazine back inside my knapsack and swung open the stall door.

But what if the Skin didn't work? I was sure I was its most challenging case. Could my dorkiness melt all of the magic?

I paused at the row of sinks and checked out my reflection in the mirror.

It was me, all right. Round face. Way-too-curly hair. So-so brown eyes and a nose that was verging on too big but, for the time being, at least, had settled for prominent. I guess my cheeks looked a little flushed from my acrobatics inside the stall, but other than that I couldn't really see the difference my mother was talking about. Any sort of supermodel effect I'd expected from the Skin definitely hadn't kicked in yet.

Bummer.

"Aren't you Sam Klein?" asked the girl standing next to me. She was tall and skinny, with dyed black hair and a nose ring.

Abby Lawton, I thought. She sat two seats away from me in geometry but hadn't spoken to me all year. She usually spent the class hunched over, peeling the black polish from her nails.

"Um, yeah," I said, surprised she even knew my name. I rarely spoke in any of my classes, but in geometry I was borderline catatonic.

"I think Kylie Frank is looking for you. I

heard something about it in the hall." She turned back to the mirror. "Cool shirt."

I stared at her. Wait, what? A compliment? Nobody at Woodlawn complimented me. They didn't *talk* to me. As far as I knew, they couldn't even see me.

Was this the Skin? Or maybe I'd misunderstood. I could be going deaf. That was definitely more believable.

I was on the verge of asking Abby to repeat herself when the second bell rang. I had about thirty seconds to get to English, otherwise Mr. Hill would lock me out. He lived for that.

I grabbed my bag and pushed my way through the door.

And that was when I heard it: "Sam Klein." Up and down the halls, the school was almost pulsing with the name. *My* name.

Sam Klein.

FOURTEEN

"Hey, that's Sam Klein, right?"

"Wait, where?"

"Oh, *that's* her."

I moved down the hall toward my locker, soaking up the attention as it swirled around me.

Of course, I assumed it was the Skin doing its thing, working its magic. I could almost feel the boost as I skipped several rungs up the Woodlawn High social ladder.

I was wrong.

People were definitely talking about me. The Abby Lawton thing hadn't been a fluke. But it wasn't because of the Skin. It was because of Kylie Frank. When the most popular girl in school demands a sit-down with a total nobody, it tends to rouse curiosity. And trigger a lot of talk.

In history, Kim Price and Georgia Beeler—soccer players who, before today, definitely had no clue who I was—approached me.

"Kylie's looking for you," Kim announced as I unpacked my bag.

"Yeah, what's up with you guys?" Georgia chimed in, eyeing me with a new, almost hungry interest. "How do you even know Kylie?"

"She, uh, lives next door to me," I explained, shrugging a shoulder and doing my best to hide my disappointment. With or without the Skin, I was still a nobody. And Kylie Frank still ruled. How could that be possible?

It was like that in every class, all day long. After a lifetime of invisible-girl status, people were finally seeing Sam Klein, only it was through the lens of their Kylie Frank worship. My newfound celebrity was simply a testament to her unflinching power-hold over the student body. I'd come to school expecting the halls of Woodlawn High to have magically transformed into a friendly neighborhood coffee shop, but it just wasn't like that. Sure, I heard my name everywhere I turned, and people constantly approached me, but it was only to ask pointed questions of the "Do you know Kylie's looking for you?" variety. There were no warm introductions or, even more disappointing, admiring glances from guys.

At least they're talking about me, I thought. *At least something's happening. No such thing as bad publicity, right?*

It was 3:10 p.m. The final bell had just rung, signaling an end to my Woodlawn High Skin debut. And I was feeling down. Not only was I wearing a magical popularity suit, but Kylie Frank's feverish Sam Klein search had also, inadvertently, triggered a viral marketing campaign. And it all amounted to a big nothing. The Sam Klein buzz around school was still more mosquito than queen bee.

I was hopeless. The pen was uncapped but the page was still empty. The redraft of my life was suffering from major writer's block.

"Well, if it isn't the girl of the hour," Gwen said, coming up behind me. "Seriously, what's going on?"

"What do you mean?" I asked carefully, shoving my head inside my locker as far as it would go. Some conversations were just best conducted without any sort of eye contact.

"I mean, why did Señora Reynolds have to pass a '*no se habla* Sam Klein' rule in my Spanish class?"

"She did?" I asked, trying to sound surprised.

Gwen nodded. "Yep. And Kylie Frank started a fire in chemistry."

"Really?" I swallowed.

"She was passing around your yearbook picture and accidentally knocked over her Bunsen burner. Mrs. Hecht had to break out the extinguisher and everything." Gwen eyed me skeptically. "Why would Kylie Frank care about you—or your yearbook picture?"

"Gee, thanks," I said, trying to look indignant despite the fact that Gwen's suspicion more than made sense. "That's a really nice thing to say."

"C'mon, Sam," she pushed. "You know what I mean."

I stared at my feet, too ashamed to tell the truth. Gwen wouldn't understand. She'd hate me.

And she'd be completely justified.

Give it back, I thought. The words flashed red through my brain. *It doesn't even work, so just give it back.*

I could have stopped it all there. I could have closed the shoe box, relinquishing my almost-hold on the stilettos. I'd taken them out for a practice spin—and fallen flat on my face. Forget Keds. I was more of an orthotics girl.

But I wasn't ready for the return. I was willing to tough it out. Blisters, calluses, the works. No pain, no gain.

I shrugged. "I have no idea. Maybe it's, like, a neighborhood thing."

Gwen stared at me pointedly, as if waiting for an "I'm a big fat liar" thought bubble to burst out of my mouth. Her eyes narrowed slightly. "Did you do something to your hair?"

"No, why?"

"I don't know," Gwen said in a voice laced with skepticism. "You just look different."

Great, I thought. *My first day in the Skin and all it gets me is twin interrogations from my mother and my best friend, two people who hate popularity about as much as I hate math.*

She glanced down at her watch. "Whatever. Let's go. I'm making osso bucco for dinner and need to stop at Whole Foods on the way home."

I took a tentative step forward, then froze as a fresh problem presented itself to me.

I couldn't go home.

Well, I could, but Kylie would definitely be waiting for me . . . and it'd be really nice to delay that particular confrontation for as long as possible. Like, till the next millennium.

"Listen," I said to Gwen. "You go ahead without me. I have some research to do in the library."

"Research? For what?"

"History," I said, talking fast. "Call me later, okay? Hope the osso-whatever turns out great."

"Uh, fine," Gwen said, squinting at me like I was some sort of strange, possibly poisonous mushroom. "I'll see you tomorrow."

I watched her walk away, feeling like something uncomfortable had just started between us. I wasn't exactly sure what it was, but I knew I was the one who'd started it.

Twenty minutes later, I was doing something I'd never, ever done before. I was attending an actual school event. Since I'd chosen randomly and said event hadn't actually started yet, I couldn't, at that moment, give any specifics. But I had a feeling whatever I was about to watch was sports-related. The fact that I was sitting in the bleachers staring at the field was a pretty big giveaway.

It wasn't like I was anti-extracurricular or anything. But freshman year Gwen had vowed never to set foot in Woodlawn High outside of mandatory school hours, and football flyers and homecoming posters just weren't the sort of thing Alex would ever notice. Since the thought of attending one of those events alone was, for obvious reasons, about as unappealing as to-furkey, I'd steered clear.

But today was different. I was wearing the Skin . . . and a watch, too. And the latter told me I had some serious time to kill. I had to be home by seven for dinner, but when I said goodbye to Gwen it was barely four. The way-too-wide window posed a serious threat to my Kylie Frank avoidance plan.

The flyers in the hall had summed up my choices: the drama club's dress rehearsal of *Our Town*, a Mathletes competition or a model Congress.

It was pretty slim pickings, which was why I'd wandered out to the field and climbed onto the bleachers, joining the definitely-cooler-than-model-Congress crowd.

And really, it's not so bad, I thought as a bunch of hot guys in cleats jogged onto the lawn. Everyone cheered.

As soon as I saw the lacrosse sticks, though, I knew I'd miscalculated. If this was a lacrosse game, surely Tanner Mullins—captain of the lacrosse team—would be playing. And, of course, his loyal girlfriend, Kylie Frank, would be watching.

As if on cue, Tanner clomped onto the field and raised his lacrosse stick high above his head. The crowd went wild.

I craned my neck and, sure enough, spotted Kylie Frank standing in the very front between

Jules and Ella. Even from a distance, I could tell something wasn't right. She wasn't smiling or cheering, and her claps were distinctly un-enthusiastic. She turned, scanning the sea of sports fans.

I should've gone with the Mathletes, I thought, shooting straight up. What was I think-ing? Tanner Mullins was a super-jock. He and Kylie were A-listers. This was their domain.

I pushed my way down the bleachers. I had about three minutes before Kylie Frank spotted me.

I was wrong. No sooner had I navigated the long line of limbs that separated me from the aisle when I ran smack into Kylie Frank.

"Where've you been?" she snapped, breath-less. Behind us, Ella and Jules stared. Ella looked concerned; Jules looked interested. "I was look-ing for you all day."

"Uh, really?" I said, wishing desperately for a trapdoor I could escape through. "I didn't know."

Kylie tossed her hair over her shoulder and shot me a *puh-lease* look. "We need to talk."

"Sure. What's up?" I asked, trying to keep my voice equal parts calm and clueless.

"Not here," Kylie said, her voice beyond an-noyed. "Someplace private."

Leaving Ella and Jules gaping in her wake, she turned and marched down the bleacher stairs. I followed her inside, legs wobbling. I was tempted to run—try to make a break for it—but it was hopeless. I couldn't outrun her. And after what I'd done, a confrontation was inevitable.

Besides, the entire school was on Sam Klein alert. If I tried to escape, I'd be blocked by one of Kylie's many minions before I even cleared the field. After all, this was her school. For years to come, Woodlawn High would remember Kylie Frank. Skin or no Skin, I was just passing through.

FIFTEEN

All in all, it was a pretty convincing performance. I'd been rehearsing the Kylie Frank confrontation in my head for going on twenty-four hours and, though I'd secretly been hoping it wouldn't happen, I felt fairly well prepared when it did.

"Give it back," Kylie said as soon as the heavy aluminum doors closed. We were standing in the hallway outside the gym. Behind us, the glass trophy case gleamed, highlighting decades of Woodlawn High victories, back to a time when the school actually had its own bowling team.

"Give what back?" I asked, wondering if

maybe I should've tried to prop the door open. I didn't want anyone to overhear our conversation, but Kylie looked furious and part of me worried she'd hit me. Her hands were bunched into tight, tiny fists and her wide eyes had taken on sort of a pogo stick effect, jumping up and down the hall with a weird speed and ferocity.

I edged back toward the door. If things got too out of control, I could just shoot out.

Kylie snorted. "Please. Don't waste my time acting all innocent and clueless. I know you have it, so just give it to me."

"Really, I wish I could help," I said, trying to keep my argument simple and on message. "But I don't know what you're talking about."

Kylie rolled her eyes. "Right." She looked at me as if trying to decide how full of it I actually was. "The *Skin*. It's gone."

"Wow, I'm really— That's awful," I said. "What happened?"

Kylie flipped her hair back indignantly. Under normal circumstances, I'm sure the move would've intimidated me to the point of admission, but today Kylie, and her hair, really weren't at their best. Both looked tired and stressed out, dingy rather than vibrant.

Was that from Skin withdrawal? I wondered. Or simply stress? Was the Skin in some way responsible for Kylie's perfect looks?

"Nothing *happened,*" she spit out. From her tone, I could tell that she'd retraced the events of last night at least a million times. "That's the thing. I took it off to shower and when I got out it was gone." Her eyes flashed over me. "And *you're* the only one who knew about it."

"Well, me and whoever it is that sent it to you in the first place," I said coolly.

Kylie blinked and I could tell there was a part of her that had considered the exact same thing.

We stood there for a few seconds, neither of us saying anything.

"I should never have told you about it," she mumbled, breaking the silence. "I broke the rules. That's why this is happening."

Rules. What were these mysterious rules? I wondered, rubbing the Skin through my shirt-sleeve. It was still there, feeling great. But would it last? Was I breaking the rules right now? I had absolutely no idea.

Then again, this really wasn't a good time to ask.

"Calm down," I told her. "I'm sure it'll turn up somewhere."

"I looked all night. It's gone." Kylie groaned. Her eyes flicked over me, and she took in my appearance for the very first time. "You look different," she announced in an accusing tone.

Her gaze dropped pointedly to my arm, as if she'd recently developed x-ray vision.

Despite the tenseness of the situation, I was tempted to roll my eyes. Unbelievable. So far the Skin had only succeeded in attracting negative attention—something I'd never needed help with before.

"I got my hair cut," I lied. "And bought some of those nose strips—you know, for blackheads?"

Kylie fixed her cool blue eyes on me but said nothing.

"Look, I wish I could help," I said, almost wincing at my insincerity. You never really know how low you can sink until you sink that much farther. "But I really can't. I mean, sure, you showed it to me that day, but other than that, I really don't know—"

"You'd better not be lying," Kylie warned. I could tell she was torn, unsure what to believe.

"I'm not," I insisted, my pulse racing. I felt sort of sweaty, too. Criminal activity was quite the workout—way more strenuous than thirty minutes on a treadmill. "But if I think of anything, I swear I'll let you know."

"Whatever," Kylie said, pushing past me. "I'm going home to look some more."

I listened to her angry steps retreat, feeling a mix of relief and fear. The confrontation was over and I'd survived. Actually, I'd won. I still had the Skin and I'd planted enough doubt in Kylie's brain that, while I was still her number-one suspect, she wasn't absolutely convinced.

But the exchange had definitely made its mark. I had no idea how life in the Skin would play out, but each scenario had its downside. If it didn't work, I was stuck with my loser self *and* a defective Skin. And if it did work, well, Kylie Frank wasn't stupid. She'd figure things out, probably sooner rather than later. And when she did, I'd have an enemy.

Who wanted to rip my Skin off.

I wandered back out to the game and watched the now mud-covered players club each other with wooden sticks. I had no idea how lacrosse was played—from what I could tell, it was a pretty brutal sport—but I was in desperate need of a distraction. And since Tanner Mullins was team captain, I could've watched for hours.

Someone blew a whistle on the field and the two teams trotted off to the sidelines. It seemed like the game was over and, based on the claps and cheers around me, Woodlawn had won. I rose to my feet, feeling a little disappointed. I could've used a few more minutes of sweat-soaked hottie watching. But it was just as well. I had to head home soon—I didn't want my parents to worry. Besides, the bleachers were emptying quickly.

"Hoping for a replay?"

I looked up. Tanner Mullins was a few rows ahead of me, packing up his sports bag. His shaggy blond hair was streaked with mud and his cheeks were still red from the game.

And he was looking at me. Yes, me.

I swallowed, waiting for the—what? Panic? Nausea? Overwhelming cramps? I'd never been in a cute-guy-talking-to-me sort of situation before, so I had no idea how I'd respond. I was pretty sure it'd be ugly.

But the humiliation and regret-triggering reaction never came. Instead, and almost involuntarily, I felt my spine straighten and my mouth curve into a smile.

"Hey," I said, in a voice so calm and relaxed Tanner Mullins could've been the checkout girl at Rite Aid. "I'm Sam Klein."

Tanner blinked. "Sam Klein. Where have I heard that before?" He shrugged. "Well, it's really cool of you to support the team. And you stayed to the end." He scanned the empty bleachers, his expression almost pouty. "Not everybody does, which is totally lame."

He's talking about Kylie, I thought.

A fresh shot of guilt twisted my stomach. But

as Tanner swung his bag over his shoulder and smiled, it melted instantaneously away.

"Listen," he said, his dimples winking at me. "I got to get cleaned up, but we have another game Thursday if you're interested. It'd be cool if you stopped by."

Was all this attention—and my calm and collected response—courtesy of the Skin? I had absolutely no idea. But whatever was happening, I liked it. A lot. And I wanted more.

I tilted my head to one side in what I hoped was an exact replica of Kylie Frank's pose in her kissing-Tanner picture. "Definitely," I said, smiling back at him. "I'm in."

SIXTEEN

*W*hen it happened the first time, I thought it was a fluke. Maybe that was stupid of me, but I couldn't help it. It was almost February and I'd spent a good solid week in the Skin, with little to no results. Sure, I'd been dealt the occasional smile in the hallway and I still had my Tanner moment to cling to, but other than that, my life really hadn't changed.

And neither had Kylie Frank's. Of course, it was hard to tell since she was as busy as ever, cheerleading and partying and color-coordinating her outfits. But I saw her in homeroom every morning, could feel her glares as she walked down the aisle toward her desk. Her suspicion hadn't ebbed, which, despite my guilt, made increasingly less sense. She was still queen and I was just a serf. The planets hadn't shifted at all.

It was disappointing, to say the least. In the Skin, I'd expected lightning-fast change. I wanted to feel it hit, pinpoint the exact moment in time. It was like choosing a crash diet over the more practical Weight Watchers. Rapid-fire results weren't just a perk, they were the main appeal.

I hadn't even lost water weight.

I was pretty sure the Skin was a dud. Still, I persevered. Stripping it off was tantamount to giving up, sealing my socially inferior fate forever. I just couldn't bring myself to do it. But my hopes were definitely dwindling. Each day that closed with my "loser Sam Klein" status still intact took a little something out of me. So when, on that cold gray morning, I walked into homeroom to find Jules Johnston perched at her desk smiling and waving at me, as warm and friendly as Oprah's wave to her studio audience, I completely froze.

Jules waved again and, after a few more shocked seconds ticked by, I pulled myself together enough to go sit down.

"So, did you hear?" Jules asked, like we'd been best friends for years. She scooted her chair over and leaned her head so close to mine I got a huge, sinus-busting whiff of her perfume. (I'd smelled it before, I remembered, in the pages of one of my magazines. The scent was so cloying I'd had to toss the entire issue.)

"Um, I don't think so," I said, wondering if Jules's peroxide abuse had finally pushed her over the edge. I still couldn't believe she was talking to me.

She smiled coyly, obviously enjoying her role as news breaker. "Kylie and Tanner had a big fight," she announced, pausing slightly for maximum drama. "Huge."

I swallowed; the weirdness of the situation temporarily forgotten. "Um, about what?"

"I heard Kylie's been blowing off Tanner's games. And she stood him up at the gym, too." She wrinkled her nose in distaste. "I tried to ask her about it, but she wouldn't talk. She's been such a freak lately I can't even deal."

"Wow, that's too bad." I shifted in my chair, trying to stay calm. It was hard, considering the fact that two overwhelming realizations had just struck. The first told me that finally—*finally*—the Skin was working. (It had to be the Skin. I knew better than to think Jules was talking to me for any other reason.) The second confirmed that I was, without a doubt, an evil, horrible person. Who else would so happily profit at someone else's expense?

"Whatever," Jules said, raising her perfectly tweezed eyebrows. "I totally saw it coming. I mean, come on. Kylie's pretty, but she's no Angelina. And Tanner's way too cool to be—" Her mouth snapped shut as Kylie and Ella walked down our row. "Okay, shhh," she warned, like I'd been the one gossiping. "To be continued."

Kylie and Ella sat down. Despite her snide remarks, Jules adhered to her regularly scheduled suck-up session, kicked off by edging her desk as close to Kylie's as possible.

"So," she said, dropping her voice to a loud, conspiratorial whisper. "You have to tell me what happened. I'm *dying*."

Kylie ran her fingers through her hair, which, I couldn't help but notice, was looking sort of flat. "Nothing to tell," she said. Her voice sounded weird, I decided. Like she was trying really hard to sound upbeat. "We got into a fight but then talked it out and now everything's back to normal."

Jules shot me a look that, thankfully, Kylie didn't catch. "Well," she said. "If that's true, I'm really glad."

Kylie swiveled around and stared pointedly at Jules. "It's true," she said crisply. "Why wouldn't it be?"

Jules's smile was pure innocence. "Of course it's true, sweetie," she said. "You said it is, so it is." She waited for Kylie to turn around, then turned to me with a "Yeah, right" look on her face.

I didn't have time to respond. Mr. Martino walked into the room and flipped open the roll book, and that was that. My friendship with Jules Johnston had begun, about as subtly as her perfume.

The next day started much the same way. And the next. After a few more homerooms passed, the image of Jules already seated, smiling and waving at me like Miss Universe, didn't cause me to freeze in my tracks. I was even able to enjoy it—and wave back.

"Great coat. Is that Miu Miu?" she asked one morning in early February.

"Uh, no," I said, distracted. What was up with her hair? The Born Blond she'd been sporting for the last week was gone, replaced by a dark chestnut. And she'd definitely spent some serious time with a curling iron that morning. The burned-looking strands had been coaxed into chunky half-spirals that extended from her scalp in stiff plaits. It was a botched job, definitely, but after a few more minutes of study, I realized what was happening.

Jules Johnston wanted dark, curly hair. Just like mine.

"Well, what is it? Marc Jacobs?" Jules guessed, staring at my down parka like Gore-Tex was the new gold. She lurched forward and grabbed it off the back of my chair. Not a single hair on her shellacked head moved.

"No," I said again, trying to pull it back.

Too late. Jules's hands ran alongside the coat's interior toward the label.

" 'Lands' End,' " she read out loud.

My stomach dropped. My short-lived friendship with Jules Johnston was definitely over. The rewrite of my life was composed in disappearing ink.

"Omigod, how cute are you?" Jules squealed. "I completely forgot about that catalog. I'm gonna check it out tonight."

Oh, come on, I thought. Magic Skin or no magic Skin, things like this just didn't happen to me. There are people who set fashions and there are people who follow them. And then there are people who are so far from doing either, they get questioned by mall security just for trying to *enter* Saks. Guess which category I belonged to?

"So is that landsend.com?" Jules asked. Her fingers hovered eagerly over her iPhone.

"Uh-huh," I said absently as Ella and Kylie made their way down the aisle and slid into their chairs.

Kylie turned around and I waited for Jules to scoot forward. Only this morning, she didn't do much of anything. Other than raising her hand in a wave so weak and painfully fake it made my toes curl, she didn't move at all.

Kylie's smile wilted. Her gaze shot between Jules and me, taking in our kissing desks and the "We're so friendly!" tilt of our heads. Her eyes settled on me and narrowed shrewdly, as if to say "You're so busted." Then she whipped back around, facing front.

Well, that's that, I thought. Any doubts Kylie had had about my thievery were gone, completely wiped away.

Still, I'd be lying if I said I wasn't excited. I couldn't help it. The Skin was working. I was on my way.

127

SEVENTEEN

*L*ater that night, I was trying—and failing—to convince myself that my geometry textbook was the latest issue of *People* when my cell phone rang.

Thank god, I thought as I raised it to my ear. I was a little surprised, since my phone lived an emergency-only sort of existence, but I figured it was Alex, checking in to see if my shape-challenged brain needed any help. "Hello?"

"Hey! Whatcha doin'?" asked the unbelievably perky voice on the other line.

I frowned. It definitely wasn't Alex. Or Gwen. Nor was it the video store, the dentist's office or a competing phone company, vying for my business. Who else could possibly be calling *me*?

"Um, a little geometry," I said, wondering if this was a wrong number and if I shouldn't just hang up now.

"Ugh, you have Slater, right? I hear he's the worst."

"Jules?" I guessed. I'd never given her my phone number, but there was always the school directory.

The mystery caller laughed. "No, but I just got off the phone with her. It's me. Heidi. Adrienne's here too."

I blinked. The only Heidi I knew, or at least knew of, was Heidi Zapler. She and her best friend, Adrienne Scott, were members of Kylie's worshipful chick clique. I'd never spoken to either of them and now they were calling me.

"Uh, hi," I managed to squeak. "What's up?"

"Oh, nothing," Heidi answered, but there was excitement in her voice. "We were just wondering if you heard."

"Heard what?" I asked as my phone clicked. I pulled it away from my ear, puzzled. Was that the battery dying?

"Kylie and Tanner are over," Heidi squealed. She sounded beyond delighted.

I swallowed. "Wait, what? I don't think I—"

Click.

It was the other line, I realized with a start. Someone else was calling for me. I had two callers. Wow.

"Hold on," I said. I spent the next few seconds staring blankly at my phone. Unsurprisingly, I'd never used call-waiting before.

"Hello?" I said, after several clumsy beeps and a few "still me"s from Heidi.

"They broke up!" cried a voice in a loud staccato burst.

"I know," I said automatically, then added: "Who is this?"

"It's Jules. How do you know?"

"Heidi's on the other line."

"Oh," said Jules, miffed at being outscooped. But she seemed to recover after a few seconds, offering a generous "Want to conference her in?"

"That's okay," I said quickly. If call-waiting was tough, I was pretty sure conferencing would kill me. "She can wait."

Jules giggled, clearly delighted. "I guess he dumped her right after final bell," she continued. "I called it, didn't I?"

"Yep," I agreed. I wasn't sure if this was actually true, nor did I care. I was too busy trying not to shout *"Yes!"* at the top of my lungs.

"I can't *believe* she tried to pretend everything

was okay when it so obviously wasn't. I mean, how desperate can you get? It's so sad."

"I know," I said, my head swimming. "Listen, I'll see you tomorrow, okay?"

"Sure," Jules said. I could hear the disappointment in her voice. "I'll tell you more in homeroom."

Dazed, I clicked back over to Heidi and told her I had to go too. Then I flipped my phone shut and flopped onto my bed.

Tanner Mullins is single, I thought as a shiver of excitement rippled down my spine. *He's single. And so am I.*

My phone rang again.

It's Tanner, I thought, snapping it open. "Hello?"

"You did this. I can't believe it!"

Oops. This time around I didn't have to ask who it was.

"Hey, Kylie," I said, trying to stay calm. "Listen, I told you the truth before, I swear. I don't know a thing about—"

"Just shut up, okay?" she seethed. "How else can you explain what's happening? Jules is suddenly your new BFF and Tanner dumps me? Please."

"Uh, I don't know," I said. *Just get off the phone and you can go back to dreaming about Tanner Mullins,* I thought. "Look, I swear I—"

"Quit wasting my time." Kylie snorted. "Just give it back and I'll forget about this whole nightmare."

"I have to go," I said quickly. "I'm really sorry you're so upset."

"Give. It. Back."

I took a deep breath and hung up.

I brushed my teeth, washed my face, plastered one of my new pore strips across my nose and stripped it off (I hadn't completely lied to Kylie). Then I crawled into bed, closed my eyes and tried not to imagine tomorrow.

It was hard.

I kept waiting for the panic to hit. Kylie was beyond furious. Still, my excitement about Tanner's new bachelor status combined with the multiple phone calls outweighed my anxiety. In the Skin, I felt protected. Except for bathing, I never took it off. (The practice might not win me any good-grooming awards, but why waste a drop of popularity?) And it was working.

If you're expecting some sort of amazing, romantic story about what happened the next morning, you're in for a serious disappointment. I know I was. I woke up half (okay, three-fourths) expecting to find Tanner Mullins waiting in the someone had broken in, but no, nothing was missing. Laptop. Notebooks. Backpack. They were all there.

I should have felt panicked. Or furious. And I definitely should have reported the incident to the principal's office. But since I was wearing the only possession I really, truly cared about, the fuss hardly seemed worth it.

The rewrite of my life was in progress—and so far it was way more exciting than any romance novel.

driveway, holding two dozen long-stemmed roses and ready for a rebound romance.

Well, that didn't happen.

I didn't even see Tanner that day. Or the next. By Thursday, I was contemplating skipping his lacrosse game when I finally caught a glimpse of him walking down the hall. He was with a few of his teammates and didn't stop to talk, but when he saw me, he smiled and—I think—winked.

A *wink*. That had to be huge, right? My own history of flirtation was nonexistent, but even so. A wink was a wink. And okay, maybe it was a little slimy, considering he and Kylie had just broken up, but that was hardly my problem, I reasoned, and therefore wasn't my place to judge.

Besides, when the captain of the lacrosse team winks at you in the hallway, you have to attend his game. I was pretty sure that was a law in several states.

So I went. I sat in the front row between Heidi and Adrienne, who, a week before, would never have made room for me on a crowded bleacher. But that afternoon they were all too eager to squeeze me in. If I'd asked, I bet they'd have built me an extra bench, too.

Heidi ran a long, thin hand through her long, thin hair, reminding me of Gwen's nickname for her, Hungry Hungry Heidi. "You have to come out with us after the game," she gushed. "The whole team heads over to Friendly's."

"We take up, like, half the tables," Adrienne added proudly, like booth hogging was an art.

"I'll think about it," I promised as the players trotted onto the field. I saw Tanner gaze up and into the crowd, his eyes moving down the bleachers in a businesslike manner. When he saw me, he smiled and gave a thumbs-up.

My mouth went dry.

That's terrible, I told myself. *You stole the Skin from Kylie and now you're ready to steal her boyfriend, too? You should feel really bad for even thinking about this stuff.*

A whistle blared, signaling the start of the game. Whenever Tanner stole the ball I clapped. When he scored, I stomped my feet and screamed his name. And even though I had absolutely no idea what was happening on the field about ninety percent of the time, I figured I covered all the really important stuff.

When the game was over (I was pretty sure that, again, Woodlawn had won, but made a mental note to do a little online lacrosse research when I got home), I really wanted to hang back and talk to Tanner—or even head over to Friendly's and wait for him—but decided against it. Kylie Frank had arrived midgame and was sitting

about ten seats away from me. She definitely had dibs.

"Listen, thanks for the invite," I told Heidi and Adrienne as we edged our way toward the aisle. "But I can't go. Maybe another time, okay?"

"You're not coming?" Heidi asked. She looked crushed. "Really?"

"We're usually there for a couple of hours," Adrienne assured me. "In case you change your mind."

"Hey, Sam! Sam Klein!"

I turned. Tanner was standing at the edge of the field, smiling. At me.

That was all it took. The dizzy feeling was back.

"Hey," I said softly, not trusting my voice.

"I heard you cheering," he said. "You're our number-one fan."

"Uh, sure am," I said.

"Listen, we have another game on Tuesday," he said, flashing me a Colgate-bright smile. "See you there?"

"Definitely."

I climbed down from the bleachers and walked into the hall, toward my locker. My Tanner high was so intense that I barely even gasped when I looked down and noticed the locker door hanging wide open.

I checked the contents, confirming that yes,

EIGHTEEN

"**9** should have her up and running in about three weeks," Alex told Gwen and me. We were in his garage, staring down at a sheet of fiberglass that was, according to his blueprints, destined to become his latest soapbox car.

I glanced around the room, at the dismantled baby carriage and cans of paint, the woodworking bench covered with tools whose names and functions I wasn't even remotely curious about, and smiled. "Not possible," I said. "I know you're good but you're not *that* good."

"Oh, Sam," Alex said, shaking his head. "You have so much to learn."

Gwen lifted her head out of *Gourmet*. "*I* think you can do it." She shot me a look. "Stranger things have been known to happen."

A tiny shiver ran down my spine. Bit by bit, the halls of Woodlawn were warming to me. I was definitely on the rise. But each inch I climbed seemed to add to the tension that had cropped up between Gwen and me. It had started that first afternoon in the hallway and, as far as I could tell, didn't plan on moving anytime soon.

Before I could answer her, my cell rang. Or rather, it started to sing. I reached into my bag and grabbed it.

Gwen groaned. "Will you please turn that thing off?" she said, plucking a screwdriver from the workbench. "Or at least switch it to vibrate?"

"Sorry," I muttered. "I'm not really sure how."

This was true. Sort of. Jules had switched my ringtone earlier that week ("Omigod, how can you *not* know this song? It totally changed my life—I'm so jealous you get to listen to it for the first time. . . .") and I really didn't know how to change it back. On the other hand—and this was something I could never admit to Gwen, especially when she was holding something sharp—I kind of liked the cheesy Top Forty song Jules had chosen.

"I'll do it," Gwen volunteered, twirling the screwdriver like a baton.

Ignoring her, I checked the screen and frowned. I didn't recognize the number but that didn't surprise me. I'd been getting so many calls lately, it was impossible to keep them all straight.

Ever since Heidi's call the week before, my phone hadn't stopped ringing. At this point, I was pretty sure I was single-handedly keeping Verizon afloat. It started in the morning with Jules's routine wake-up-what-are-you-wearing-are-you-sure-you-don't-need-a-ride call, followed by a steady stream of random invitations, check-ins and late-breaking gossip. Each time I answered, I felt a new thrill of excitement.

"Hello?" I said.

"Hey, sweetie! What's up?" asked a high-pitched female voice. Without waiting for a response, it continued. "Listen, I talked to everyone else and they totally agree. You *have* to join."

"Wait, who—"

"I mean, I can't believe it's taken this long. Pep squad needs you! I'm sure you already know this but we practice Mondays, Wednesdays and Fridays, so just come to the gym after final bell tomorrow. You don't need to audition or anything, isn't that great?"

"Uh, yeah," I said, my head spinning. Pep squad? I was actually being asked to join pep squad—a serious A-list club reserved for the perfectly shaped, toned and color-coordinated. I'd never been invited to join *anything*—not even lame clubs like the calligraphy society or academic decathlon.

You can't even box-step without tripping, whispered a little voice inside my head.

I rubbed my arm, feeling the Skin underneath my cotton shirt.

My stomach curled with excitement. It would be okay. The Skin would make sure of it.

"Hey," I said into the phone. "Thanks a lot—I mean, that's really great news. But, um, who is this?"

A giggle shot straight through the receiver, piercing my ear. "Oh my god, you're too funny. It's Gina! Listen, I have to call Jules back. She wanted to tell you the news but since I'm a co-captain I totally pulled rank." Gina laughed again. "She was *so* pissed. See you tomorrow, sweetie!"

I snapped the phone shut. Gwen and Alex were staring at me.

"Who was that?" Gwen asked.

"Let me guess," Alex said, his face closed. "Tanner Mullins needs you to spot him."

Ever since I'd started attending lacrosse

games, Alex's teasing had become relentless. He'd diagnosed me with a deep-seated and potentially fatal case of mimbo—male bimbo—obsession, and brought it up whenever possible. It was beyond annoying, especially since Tanner and I weren't even going out. Or anything. I just liked to watch him play. He was, after all, team captain. And though I knew absolutely nothing about lacrosse, even I could tell he was gifted. What was so wrong about supporting local talent?

But no matter how many times I explained this, Alex wouldn't stop. Obviously, he hated Tanner just because he was a jock, which was wrong on so many levels I couldn't stand it.

My cheeks turned bright red. "Shut up. It was Gina Yonas."

"Who's that?" Alex asked. Was it my imagination or did he look relieved?

"Gina Yonas?" Gwen cut in before I had a chance to answer. "Since when do you even know Miss Pep?"

I shrugged. "I know her. We have PE together."

"Okay, let me rephrase," Gwen said slowly, placing a hand on her hip. A glint of challenge flickered across her face. "Since when does Gina Yonas know *you*?"

Gwen had a point. Gina Yonas and I had played

basketball, volleyball and soccer together for six straight months. But through all that dribbling, passing and kicking, we'd never actually exchanged a single word. And now she was lobbying to get me into pep squad. Even I found the situation slightly perplexing—and I was wearing the Skin. From where Gwen and Alex were standing it must have looked positively *Twilight Zone.*

"I mean it, Sam," Gwen pushed. "Will you please tell us what's going on?"

I blinked. "Nothing. I mean, she wants me to join pep squad. It's really not a big deal. I don't even know—"

Gwen flashed me a serious cut-the-crap look. "Oh, please. Like you haven't noticed you're Woodlawn's 'flavah of the month'? I find that really hard to believe."

"I'm s-sorry," I stammered as heat rushed into my cheeks. "I don't know—"

"Leave her alone," Alex cut in. He turned to Gwen. "Why do you care so much anyway?"

Gwen's face closed. "I don't. It's just weird, that's all."

I stared at my feet and tried to send Alex a telepathic thanks.

"So," Gwen said after a few seconds of uncomfortable silence. "Are you gonna join?"

I blinked, my thoughts too jumbled to form any sort of connection with Alex. "Join what?"

Gwen rolled her eyes. "Pep squad, dummy. Are you gonna go all A-W-E-S-O-M-E on us?"

Even though I knew she was being sarcastic, Gwen's words caused a little flutter kick in my stomach. I was excited. I couldn't help it.

"I'm thinking about it," I mumbled. I glanced between Alex and Gwen. "Will you guys hate me?"

Alex smiled. "Do what you want." He looked at Gwen, his face hard. "Right?"

Gwen rolled her eyes again. "Whatever." She turned to me. "If you want to explore the world of the barely-there skirt, be my guest." She scooped her bag off the floor. "Listen, I gotta get dinner ready. I'll talk to you guys later."

Watching her go, I felt a pang of anxiety followed swiftly by annoyance. Maybe I was a cheat and a thief, but did Gwen have to be so judgmental? It wasn't like I was making her join pep squad with me. Why did she care what I did? She had her cooking. Alex had his cars. Couldn't I have something too?

And why were my friends the only two people in school who seemed completely impervious to the Skin? The rest of Woodlawn thought I could do no wrong.

Gwen and Alex don't care about popularity, I realized suddenly. *The Skin can't touch them because they don't believe in what it has to offer.*

"I don't know why she's so mad," I muttered.

Alex lowered the fiberglass to the workbench and grabbed a pair of safety goggles. "You know Gwen. She lives to get riled up about this stuff. She'll calm down."

"I guess," I said.

He looked at me. "Seriously, Sam, if you want to do this, you should." He smiled. "I'll even go to your first game."

"Thanks," I said. I tried to picture Alex crammed into the bleachers, hooting with the rest of the fans, but my brain refused to cooperate. I guess some things are just too weird, even for the imagination.

Twenty minutes later, I was walking home from Alex's house when my backpack started singing. I reached in and grabbed my cell phone. It was Gwen.

"Look, about before," she said as soon as I answered. "I was way too harsh. Just because I have no interest in pep squad, I know you think that stuff's important, so I'm happy for you. Really. I hope all your dreams come true, even if they are so painfully *High School Musical.*"

"Uh, thanks," I said, knowing this was the

closest thing to an apology I was ever going to get.

"Seriously, Sam," Gwen continued. "I hope you get to do all the things you've been talking about forever. Like go to Spring Fling and win the crown or ribbon or wand—or whatever stupid, sexist trinket they dispense as a symbol of a girl's total self-worth. I really do."

"As long as you're not mad," I said.

"I'm not. I guess I'm just surprised. I mean, you realize this totally blows my high school theory."

"What do you mean?"

"I mean you're amazing," Gwen explained. I could hear her clanging pots around in the background. "I've always known it. And we both know Alex does too. I just can't believe all those idiot A-listers are finally wising up."

"Uh, thanks," I said. "But just 'cause I'm joining pep squad or hanging out with new people . . . that doesn't make, I mean, nothing has to change, right? Not with us."

"Oh, I'm not worried," Gwen said, maybe a little too quickly. She'd started to pound something and her voice was choppy and breathless. "I was never worried about that."

My other line beeped.

"I should go," I said. "Thanks for calling. I'll talk to you tomorrow."

As Gwen hung up, a part of me wondered if I should have stayed on the line with her a little longer. Just to make sure we were okay.

Then the other line rang again and a shot of that new, who-could-it-be excitement coursed through me.

Forget it, I told myself as I clicked over. *There wasn't anything left to say.*

NINETEEN

"I'm not so sure about this," I said, staring down at the two strips of navy and yellow fabric that comprised my new pep squad uniform. By some geometric feat, the ensemble was supposed to cover my body without triggering an arrest for indecent exposure, but I honestly couldn't see how.

Don't panic, I thought. *You suck at geometry.*

"Oh, stop," Jules said, forcing her freshly dyed and curled chestnut hair into a high ponytail. "You're gonna look hot."

"And don't worry," Gina squealed, giving my

arm a playful smack. "It's so comfy, you're gonna want to wear it all the time."

I bit my lip to keep from saying "It's just perfect for my favorite nude beach" and settled for a smile instead.

It was my first day as an official member of Woodlawn High's pep squad, and I couldn't shake the queasy feeling that was steadily climbing up my stomach and into my throat. All afternoon I'd focused on my clumsiness and complete lack of coordination, but now, staring down at my postage stamp–sized uniform, I realized I had even bigger issues.

Skin or no Skin, my body was far from perfect. And the skimpy pep squad garb was hardly forgiving.

I tried to console myself with the fact that everyone else on the squad would be wearing the same outfit. They had to feel equally self-conscious, right?

No, I thought as my eyes swept the locker room, taking in nothing but toned abs, sinewy limbs and perky everything. I was surrounded by perfection.

My gaze fell on a corner of the room where Kylie and Ella were quietly unpacking their gym bags. Kylie's long blond hair was pulled back in a neat twist as she and Ella talked softly, completely removed from the rest of the group. She looked pale, I decided. And a little thinner than usual, though I couldn't be sure since she was still wearing the sweatpants she'd worn today.

Since when does Kylie Frank wear sweatpants to school? I wondered.

She turned her head and shot me a mean look, as if she'd heard my thoughts.

My heart thumped. This was yet another aspect of pep squad I'd overlooked. Kylie Frank was on the team. She was, if memory served, a cocaptain. Ever since her call, I'd managed to steer pretty clear of her. Other than homeroom, where I was protected by a close-clinging Jules, we didn't have any classes together. Even so, I knew she was still furious about the Skin. I saw it in her eyes whenever we passed each other in the hall—accusation mingled with frustration since, despite my social rise, she still had no concrete proof.

Well, it didn't matter anyway. Once I slipped on that rubber band of a uniform, it was all over. Every known flaw on my body—along with some I'd yet to discover—would be on display. I'd be the laughingstock of Woodlawn High. Cellulite trumped magic any day of the week.

"I can't believe Kylie even bothered to show," Jules whispered, interrupting my thoughts. She raised her finger and drew an air circle by her head. "I swear, I think she's totally lost it."

"I know," Gina added. "You should have seen the *fit* she threw when we all voted you on the squad. It was *so* weird."

"Uh, listen," I said, scooping up my things, "I'll meet you out there, okay?"

Without waiting for a reply, I headed straight for the bathroom. Changing in the stall would delay my practically nude debut by—what, thirty seconds? Maybe a minute.

It wasn't much, but I'd take what I could get.

Beauty is in the eye of the beholder, I whispered to myself, ignoring the fact that, in my particular situation, the beholders happened to be perfectly sculpted.

I changed quickly, then walked out and studied my reflection in the full-length mirror. The situation wasn't good. The pep squad uniform stretched uneasily over my body, bunching up around the hips, and the bandeau top had clearly been designed with the words *heaving* and *bosom* in mind. Unfortunately, my chest was heave-free.

All in all, I wasn't looking too sexy. I was making my way back to my locker, contemplating whether or not to change back into my regular and blissfully concealing clothes when I heard a shriek followed by a painfully loud *"What are you doing?"*

The entire pep squad, myself included, raced into the bathroom, following the screams.

Heidi Zapler was standing in front of an open stall, adjusting her skirt. A pink-faced Kylie Frank stood next to her.

Adrienne rushed over and looped her arm around Heidi's shoulder. "What happened? Are you okay?"

"She was watching me," Heidi said, pointing at Kylie. "While I—*you know.* I looked up and she was right there, staring in from the other stall." She shook her head in disbelief. "She must have been standing on the toilet or something."

The room fell silent as everyone mentally sketched the scene.

After a few seconds passed, Adrienne turned to Kylie. "Are you insane?"

Kylie's eyes flickered over me, then away. And in that second, I knew what had happened. She had assumed I'd stepped into the stall to go to the bathroom, and hoped to launch a surprise attack just as I was wiggling out of the Skin.

Only somehow she'd chosen the wrong toilet.

"I knew you were crazy," Jules huffed, glaring at Kylie like she was the clearance bin at Kmart. "But I can't believe you're a Peeping Tom. That's really sick."

"You could probably sue," Adrienne told

Heidi, who looked like she was trying really hard to cry.

Ella stepped forward. "Okay, enough," she said. "I'm sure there's a reasonable explanation for all of this." She turned to Kylie, hopeful. "Right?"

Kylie stared at her feet. She'd been caught red-handed, looking for the Skin. It belonged to her and she wanted it back. But there was really no way to communicate any of this without coming off as more insane than ever.

I could've answered for her. Right then I could've stepped up and told the truth.

But I didn't. I just stood there, waiting along with everyone else.

"She can't be here," Kylie said suddenly, her eyes flashing over me.

"What?" Gina said. "What are you even talking about?"

Jules snickered. "Wow. Talk about psycho."

"Not without trying out," Kylie continued, ignoring Jules. "You have to audition to join the squad."

I held my breath as a dozen pairs of eyes turned to me—and my ill-fitting ensemble.

"What's the big deal?" Adrienne said, Kylie's stalker moment temporarily forgotten. "We're all fine with Sam joining. Why waste time with a tryout?"

"Yeah," Gina agreed. She turned to me and smiled encouragingly. "You look great."

"Told you," Jules said smugly.

I smiled. I couldn't help it. I wasn't trying to bait Kylie, honestly. The whole scene was just too ridiculous. I looked about as cute as a hit-and-run. I almost wished Gwen were there. Almost.

A muscle in Kylie's jaw flexed. "Well, I'm a captain and I say she has to audition."

"Well, I'm a captain too," Gina countered, tossing her head back. "And I say it's fine."

Kylie glared at me as Ella stepped forward. "Come on," Ella urged her friend. "It's just pep squad. Let it go."

"Besides," Gina said, eyebrows arching into half-moons. "I don't think you're in any position to talk about the rules."

Kylie pursed her lips. Her eyes were bright and shiny, and I could tell she was fighting back tears. "Fine. Have it your way." She turned on her heel and stalked out of the room.

I watched the door swing shut behind her. Nobody said a word, and after a few more seconds, Ella turned and followed.

"God, they're such drama queens," Adrienne said, even though both Ella and Kylie had, in my opinion, been pretty calm.

"Well, I'm not standing anywhere near

Kylie," Heidi said, sniffing loudly to remind everyone of her traumatic experience. "It just doesn't feel safe."

A few of the girls reached over to pat her arm.

"Okay, people," Gina announced. "Let's head out. We're already behind schedule, thanks to little Miss Freak Show."

I followed the group out to the gym, trying really hard not to replay the scene in my head and shoving my guilt into a tiny, easily ignored corner of my brain. More than anything, I felt relief. Okay, relief mingled with excitement. I'd narrowly escaped what could have been the end of a new and improved me, and had literally bared all to my new teammates. And they'd been completely supportive and accepting. No lectures on the importance of a carb-free diet, no personal trainer recommendations. Nothing.

Maybe I don't look so bad after all, I thought as I grabbed a sweatshirt off the bench. *I can be so hard on myself sometimes.*

Jules stretched her arm around my shoulder and smiled. "Listen, I have to ask you something," she whispered conspiratorially.

My stomach twisted. Was it that obvious something was going on between Kylie and me?

"Uh, sure," I said, trying hard to sound calm. "Go ahead."

Jules leaned in closer. "So, um, where'd you

get that?" She pointed to the sweatshirt wrapped around my waist. "Is that Lands' End too? I didn't see it in the catalog."

I smiled, grateful for the distraction. I didn't deserve it, but at the moment, I didn't really care.

TWENTY

I've never wondered about my death. I don't have a goth bone in my body. But as I stood in the middle of the gym, surrounded by human Slinkys, the mystery was solved. Pep squad was going to kill me.

It was only fifteen minutes into practice and my muscles wouldn't stop twitching. My stomach felt like it was about to burst too.

A quick glance around the room confirmed that I was the only one panting. The other pep-sters looked rosy-cheeked and healthy as they cheerfully twisted their bodies into painful-looking shapes and angles. It was like they were reenacting entire chapters from my geometry text.

Talk about an obtuse angle, I thought, staring at Adrienne as she snapped her leg above her head in a move I was pretty sure qualified as torture in any country.

"Lighten up! Brighten up! Sparkle and shine! The Wolverine guys are looking mighty fine!"

Oh my. If the moves didn't kill me, the cheers would definitely do the job.

Gina wove her way through the yawning, flexing bodies that lined the mats. She stopped directly in front of me.

"Okay, ladies!" she shouted, clapping. She wasn't even the slightest bit winded. "Backbend time! Gotta limber up those spines!"

Everyone around me drifted gracefully to the mats. There were no agonized groans, no flying limbs, no Tourette's-style expletives.

"How'd you do that?" I asked Jules, who was next to me, shaped like a giant *C.*

"It's easy," she said, twisting her head around in a perfect imitation of the old *Exorcist* movie. "Just give it a try."

I lowered my body to the mat, placed my hands above my head and curled my back. Then I tried to lift up. I got about two inches off the ground before I fell like a collapsing bridge.

I regret everything I've ever eaten, I thought, staring up at the ceiling.

"Ow! Owwwww!"

It took me a minute to realize that I wasn't the one shouting in pain. I scrambled to my feet and glanced across the room, where Adrienne was hopping up and down, rubbing her head. Kylie Frank stood next to her on the mat, looking apologetic.

"I'm sorry," she said. "I just—I guess I lost my balance."

Adrienne scowled. "How can you lose your balance doing a backbend?"

Easily, I thought, though I bit my lip and kept quiet.

Adrienne turned to address the room. "She rolled into me and knocked me down." She pointed an accusing finger at Kylie. "On purpose."

"I did not!" Kylie cried. "I told you. I lost my balance." Her eyes met mine and narrowed slightly. "I was just having a little trouble focusing."

Gina placed her hands on her hips. "Maybe you should sit this one out," she said to Kylie.

Kylie shook her head. "But it was an accident," she insisted.

Jules snorted. "Right. Like your Peeping Tom episode was an accident, too."

Kylie looked around the room, absorbing the hostile laughter and cold stares. Her gaze circled back to Gina. "Fine. You're right. I'll sit this one out. And the next one too. I *quit*."

"You know what?" Ella said lightly, stepping forward to stand next to Kylie. "I've always hated pep squad." She smiled. "So I guess I quit too."

Together, they turned and walked out of the room.

"I can't believe they just *deserted* the team like that," Jules said after they were gone. "I mean, it's midseason."

"Whatever. Ella pretty much sucked anyway," Gina said. "And as far as I'm concerned, Kylie's totally let herself go. I'm not surprised she fell. I mean, I don't think she works out at all anymore."

A horrified shudder swept the room.

"Okay, people," Gina shouted, stamping her foot. "Let's get back to work! Show me how you bend those backs!"

Oh no, I thought as everyone around me fell to without so much as a groan. *Not again.*

I stretched out on the mat, placed my hands on either side of my head and pushed myself up. It wasn't exactly a backbend—my spine was still straight and I was fairly certain I looked like a coffee table—but at least I was up.

"Great work, Sam!" Gina shouted. "Fantastic!"

Okay, I thought. Clearly, I wasn't made of Silly Putty like the rest of the group, but there was no need to rub it in. I shot her a look. She smiled and gave me a thumbs-up.

"You're doing great," she whispered, then moved away to lead the squad in a rousing rendition of *Hustle hustle, use your muscle!*

I stared after her as her lean, tanned legs moved away. She actually meant it? How was that even possible?

I glanced down at my aching body. It was the Skin, of course. If I closed my eyes I could feel it working, tingling and powerful against my overtaxed limbs.

Or maybe that was just another muscle spasm.

"Uh, Sam? Need some help?"

I blinked. Jules was hovering over me, arm extended. Loud, atonal music filled the room as the rest of the squad stood, twisting and turning like windmills.

"No thanks," I said, heaving myself up. "I got it."

"You're such a natural," she said. "*So* much better than Kylie."

I found that hard—okay, impossible—to believe, but after my failed backbend I needed all the support I could get.

"Thanks," I said.

I spent the next twenty minutes trying to

mimic Jules's moves, pumping my arms, kicking my legs and, when absolutely necessary, breaking out the jazz hands. But no matter how hard I tried, everything I did was slightly off. My leaps were late and unimpressive. My twirls almost caused a domino-style crash with several of my teammates. And even though my body was doing plenty of shaking and wiggling, I was pretty sure it was doing so in all the wrong places.

"The net is open, the hoop is hot . . . come on, Wolverines, make that shot!"

They're definitely trying to kill me, I thought as I mimed a slam dunk that barely would've reached the top of a Little Tikes hoop.

"Nice work, ladies!" Gina shouted, turning off the techno music. "Looking good! Let's hit those showers!"

I bit my lip and waited for someone—anyone—to faint onto the mat. I didn't want to be the first. After a few seconds, I noticed that nobody else in the room looked like they were in desperate need of a stretcher and some CPR. Several of the girls, like Adrienne and Heidi, had actually opted to extend the workout and were jogging in place.

"Uh, Sam?" Gina said. Her face was serious and completely sweat-free. "Can you hang back for a few minutes?"

Great. Cut from the team after only one

practice. I guess there are some things even a magical Skin can't cure. Like flab and an overall lack of rhythm.

As the rest of the squad made their way to the lockers I hobbled to the front of the room where Gina was waiting.

"How'd you like practice?" Gina asked brightly, clearly choosing to ignore the pained expression on my face and the fact that I'd sweated through my uniform.

"Uh, it was great," I said carefully. I didn't want to sound too enthusiastic, considering I was about to be axed.

"So listen, I know it's early," Gina said. "But with Kylie gone, there's an opening for co-captain and I was thinking you'd be great."

I stared at Gina for several seconds to be absolutely sure this was real and not some sort of endorphin-induced hallucination. "Wow . . . but I don't think I'm really ready—"

"You'll be *great*," Gina said. She waved her hand through the air as if wiping away my anxiety. "We'll have so much fun too! Of course, I have to clear the nomination with the rest of the squad, but I really don't think that'll be a problem."

I smiled weakly.

"And we're always looking for new cheers,"

Gina continued. "So definitely let us know if you think of any."

Get out of this. This so isn't you.

I opened my mouth, but the words froze in my throat. The thought fell away, replaced by images of me, front and center in the Woodlawn yearbook. And on the field at games, smiling and waving to an admiring crowd. And in friendship collages, like the ones that lined Kylie's walls.

Why can't *this be me?* I wondered. Everything came at a price. Sure, I'd never imagined popularity's price tag included house music and a bare midriff, but some things are out of our hands.

Have some faith in yourself, I thought. *Or in the Skin.*

Was there even a difference anymore?

"Sounds great," I told Gina, though my voice sounded as wobbly as my legs. "I can't wait."

TWENTY-ONE

"*E*www!" shrieked Heidi as she watched Thad Rubin dunk his head into a huge bowl of spaghetti and wiggle it around. "That's disgusting!"

Thad lifted his tomato-stained face out of the bowl and turned to Tanner Mullins. "Dude. You owe me ten bucks."

Tanner made a big show of snapping open his wallet and pulling out the bill. "Here ya go, man. That's some hard-earned cash."

I laughed along with everyone else, but I really wasn't paying attention. For the first time ever, I was eating lunch at the A-list table. They were all there: Jules, Gina and the rest of pep squad . . . along with Tanner Mullins and his jock crew.

It was pretty thrilling.

I hadn't done it on purpose. Until today, I'd always sat with Gwen and Alex. But when the bell rang for lunch, Gina and Jules were perched by my locker door, waiting for me. We walked to the cafeteria together, and after that it just seemed like the natural thing to do.

I was having a great time too. I know the words *cafeteria* and *glamour* don't really go together, but that was how it felt. My eyes swept the room, knowing that almost everyone was wondering what was going on at my table. I'd wondered myself, just a few weeks ago.

Of course, ever since I'd sat down I could feel Gwen and Alex watching me. Without even looking at them, I·could see the expressions on their faces: hers was harsh and critical, his was baffled.

Whatever, I thought. *Don't let this ruin your lunch. You're allowed to sit anywhere you want.*

I made a mental note to call Gwen that night.

"Hey, Sam," Tanner said, snapping me back to reality. "You coming to the game tomorrow?"

He really is so cute, I thought. "Wouldn't miss it," I squeaked.

He stood and grabbed his tray. The entire row

of jocks did the same. "I'm gonna hit the gym," he announced to the table at large. As he turned, he flashed me a smile and my heart fluttered. "See ya around, Sam."

I watched him walk away. I wasn't sure what a swoon was exactly, but I was pretty sure I was on the verge.

"Oh wow, he's *so* into you," Jules informed me as she patted her curls. "It's awesome."

"Who knows," I said. But the whole nonchalance thing was hard to pull off when all I really wanted to do was scream.

I rubbed the Skin through my shirt. *Thank you,* I thought. *Thank you so much.*

I woke up the next morning with a smile on my face and the Skin stuck to my body. When I tried to slip it off for my usual lightning-fast shower, I couldn't.

At first, I thought I was just sore from another merciless pep squad practice. After three hours of jumping, kicking and twirling, every single one of my muscles had rebelled to the point of civil war. Even my elbows hurt. I'd barely been able to climb into bed the night before.

Anyone who's ever made fun of cheerleading has obviously never tried to do a left Herkie (and no, that's not some sort of variation on jerk chicken, in case you're wondering).

I reached up behind my back and tried again, tugging at the zipper. This time it slid grudgingly down my back. But when I tried to slip my arms out, the Skin wouldn't move. It had sealed somehow while I was sleeping. I'd been laminated overnight.

Okay, don't panic, I ordered myself.

I tugged at my arms.

"Ouch," I said. The Skin was definitely coming off, but—*ow*—it felt like a giant Band-Aid was being ripped from my body. My whole body. Slowly and with maximum hair-stickage.

This wasn't right. The Skin had gone from smooth as silk to extreme control-top in less than twenty-four hours. How was that even possible? It definitely wasn't a weight-gain thing. After last night's torture session, I couldn't have gained an ounce. A quick visit with my bathroom scale confirmed as much. I'd actually lost half a pound, thank you very much.

Still, there had to be some sort of explanation. The Skin had felt fine yesterday, even during prime pep hours. Or maybe that was the problem. Maybe the Skin was as out of shape as I was.

I wrenched my body with one final and

incredibly painful twist, and the Skin came loose. I rolled it off and rubbed my bright red arms and legs. I'd heard one had to suffer to be beautiful, but that was nothing compared to what popularity put you through. The Skin made a bikini wax feel like a tickle session.

Don't think about it, I thought as I tucked the Skin into the shoe box and headed for the bathroom. *Everything's falling into place. You're popular. Woodlawn loves you.*

Besides, I reasoned, it was stupid to beat myself up with questions I'd never be able to answer. I didn't have the user's manual. After my failed Google search, I'd visited Wikipedia and scoured my magazine collection, hoping to unearth some sort of Skin-related intelligence. But nothing turned up. And I couldn't, for obvious reasons, ask Kylie for pointers. That meant the niggling worry in the back of my mind—the one that proposed a link between the new pore-stifling Skin and my overall vileness—could never be confirmed.

And for that, I was just a little bit thankful.

Twenty minutes later, I'd showered, changed and slid back into the Skin. (Why was it hard to take off but still so easy to slip on? That made absolutely no sense.) It felt a little tighter than usual, so I did a few deep knee bends. Maybe it could be stretched, like just-washed jeans. Then I grabbed my bag and rushed down the stairs.

I stopped breathing somewhere around the last step.

Tanner Mullins's bright red Mustang convertible was parked in my driveway. He was in the driver's seat, adjusting something on his dashboard. When he looked up, he smiled at me.

My stomach jumped as I cast a quick, panicked glance toward the kitchen. I had maybe twenty seconds before my parents noticed me or (yikes) the yummy boy decorating their front lawn.

I opened the front door and, as softly as I could, pulled it closed. Meet the parents definitely wasn't happening today.

"Hey," Tanner said, rolling down his window as I approached. His blond hair flopped across his forehead, casual but perfect. In the morning light his blue eyes looked, if possible, even bluer than usual.

"Hi," I said, chewing on my lower lip.

Tanner settled back into his seat and smiled again.

I waited for an explanation. Something about ditching Kylie and being hopelessly, completely in love with me. Or perhaps the slightly less dramatic "I was in the neighborhood and thought you might want a ride."

Nothing happened. After a few seconds, Tanner popped the locks and turned his eyes back to me, expectant.

I walked around to the passenger seat and got in.

"Um, nice car," I said as he shifted into reverse and edged out of the driveway.

He frowned. "You think? I might trade it in for an XTerra." He checked his reflection in the rearview mirror and smoothed his hair. "I'm not really sure the whole windswept thing is working for me anymore."

"Oh no, it's great," I assured him, hating the thin, simpering sound of my voice.

He smiled. "Cool. Thanks."

Okay, clearly Tanner's agility on the lacrosse field didn't extend to the art of conversation. On the other hand, it was the first time we'd hung out for longer than three minutes, so I had to cut the guy a break. And not just because of his perfect smile and impossibly cute dimples.

"So listen," he said, turning in to the parking lot. (We were at school already? How was that even possible?) "I was thinking maybe we could go out tonight." He winked. "You know, as sort of a thank-you for supporting the team."

"Oh. Cool," I managed to gulp. I forgot about Kylie. I forgot about the Skin. I forgot about the fact that it was Thursday and no way would my parents let me go out with a guy they didn't know (and who didn't drive a hybrid and, I'd be willing to bet, wasn't familiar with even the most basic ground rules for recycling). None of it mattered. Tanner Mullins and not fainting. At that moment, those were the only things I cared about.

"Cool," Tanner repeated as his eyes swept the parking lot. His face brightened as his gaze fell on a group of letter jacket–clad guys. "Yo, butt cheese!" he yelled, opening his door. "You suck!" He turned to me. "So I'll catch up with you later, okay? I gotta go pound some sense into those boys."

"Sure," I said. "No problem."

I got out of the car and headed toward the front door just as Jules climbed out of the silver BMW she'd received for her sixteenth birthday.

"Oh wow," she breathed, her eyes wide. "Tell me you didn't just get out of Tanner Mullins's car."

"Uh, actually I did," I said, allowing myself a tiny, quasi-smug smile.

"Nice," she squealed and, of course, tacked on an "I called it, didn't I?" She smirked. "He asked you out, right? I heard he was going to."

I turned to her, surprised. "Really? You knew?" How did Jules manage to log so many hours at the hair salon and still have time left over to gossip *and* go to school?

"Uh-huh," Jules said, holding the door open for me as we walked into the building. "Who do you think gave him your address?" Jules giggled. "I wonder if Kylie saw you guys. She was probably spying on you through the window. What a fur-reak."

A fresh stab of guilt churned my stomach. No relief. No pleasure. Just pure, well-deserved guilt.

And when I rounded the corner to find Gwen and Alex waiting for me in front of my locker, the feeling only intensified.

They'd stopped by my house this morning to pick me up. Just like they did every day. Only this morning, I wasn't there. I'd completely blown them off. And, I realized in a horrified flash, I'd never called either of them last night to explain about lunch. It was totally on my list, but I'd had so many other calls to make. . . .

I had some serious apologizing to do. I didn't really feel like doing it in front of Jules, but there was no time to get rid of her.

Jules followed my gaze, her expression darkening. I could tell that she didn't approve of my old friends—and the feeling was definitely mutual. Still, when she spoke her voice was carefully noncommittal and envy-free. "Oh, look. It's Gail and Alvin."

I didn't bother to correct her. "I'm so sorry," I started in as we approached the locker.

"Well, that's great," Gwen said, her voice sharp. "But you know, you might want to call your parents. They had no idea where you were either."

"I, uh, left a little early. They weren't up yet." Okay. Half true and half not. Maybe the sentences would sort of cancel each other out. I leaned forward to open my locker. "Look, I really am sorry. You know, you could've called me if you were so worried."

"I *tried*. Your phone was turned off and your voice mail was full." She turned to Jules, her face closed. "So listen, are you gonna pick her up from now on? Because I'd appreciate a little notice."

Jules smirked. "Don't look at me," she said.

"Tanner picked me up," I said quietly. I drove my gaze straight down into the linoleum but it didn't really work. I could still feel Gwen and Alex staring at me, their expressions surprised and judging.

Alex grabbed his backpack from the floor. "I gotta get to class."

"Bye, guy," I said, tapping him on the back as he walked away.

Gwen glared at me.

"What?" I asked. God, why couldn't she just let this one go? She made such a big deal about *everything*.

"You know," she said slowly, "there's clue-less . . . and then there's just plain old dumb." She shook her head. "Have a nice life, Sam."

"Omigod, I can't believe she actually said that to you," Jules said as Gwen pushed past us. "That was so rude. I mean, what was that even *about*?"

"I don't know," I told her. It was a lie, of course. I knew exactly why Gwen was mad. And I also knew I deserved it.

TWENTY-TWO

My mother was waiting for me when I got home after school. I had just enough time to give my still-pepped-out shoulder muscles a quick squeeze, grab a few Frookies (fake Oreos supposedly sweetened with fruit juice but with an aftertaste closer to Pepto) and brainstorm some possible excuses for why I absolutely had to go out on a school night, and then she pounced.

"*What* is this?" she asked, waving a fragrant piece of wax paper in my face.

I blinked, remembering. After pep squad, Jules, Gina and a few of my other new A-list BFFs had headed over to Wendy's to eat. And once I sat down with my burger and fries, everyone else hopped aboard the cellulite train, expanding their "Diet Coke only" orders to include onion rings, fries and—oh my!—even the occasional Frosty.

I thought I'd buried the evidence in the trash as soon as I got home, but obviously I hadn't done a very good job.

I swallowed my last bite of Frookie. "It was just a burger," I said, trying to keep my voice light. "A plain burger. I stayed away from the Baconator and didn't even have dessert."

My mother looked at me as if I'd just suggested we open a food court in our living room. "That," she said, placing a judgmental hand on her hip, "is completely beside the point and you know it."

"It's really not a big deal."

"Who are you?" my mother snapped. "Because you're certainly not my daughter. *My* daughter knows that chomping on one fast-food burger is the equivalent of eating fifty-five square feet of rain forest. That's almost the size of our kitchen, Sam!"

"It really wasn't that filling," I muttered, but realized it was a mistake as soon as the words came out of my mouth.

My mother's face twisted with anger.

I swung my bag over my shoulder and headed for the stairs, hoping to avoid the imminent lecture. "Listen, I'm not gonna be here for dinner. I have to meet some friends at the library. We're doing a report for history."

"Report? What report?"

Good question. I really hadn't had time to come up with anything specific. I reached the top of the stairs and turned slowly around, hoping the altitude change would trigger a strike of genius. "That's what we're trying to figure out." I took a deep breath and exhaled yet another lie. "I was thinking the whole ethanol debate might be the way to go."

My mother frowned. "I don't know," she said slowly. "It's a school night."

"Well, it's a *school* project." *Oh please say yes,* I silently begged. *I know I'm evil and heinous— the sort of person who exploits the environment to forward her own petty social agenda—but please don't let that come between me and my date with Tanner Mullins.*

"Okay," my mother said, after several seconds. "But I want you home as soon as the library closes."

"Definitely!" I said, making a mental note to find out exactly what time that was.

I closed my bedroom door behind me, then took off my clothes. After a solid ten minutes of hopping, tugging and wriggling in what I'm sure would have impressed onlookers as a spot-on imitation of a Mexican jumping bean, I was out of the Skin and in the shower, wondering whether compulsive lying ran in my family or if, lucky me, I was a Klein original.

I slipped—again, easily—back into the Skin and squirted myself with body spray. Still petrified to actually wash the Skin but even more petrified of smelling like the wrestling team, I'd settled for the bath-in-a-bottle alternative. It was definitely the Carpet Fresh approach to personal hygiene, but it was the best I could do.

I pulled on a fresh pair of jeans and what I hoped was a loose-in-a-sexy-sort-of-way T-shirt, and stepped lightly down the stairs to avoid another run in with my mom.

"Sam!"

Obviously my sneaky walk needed a little practice. I turned around, trying hard to keep my face clear of any sort of expression that screamed "I'm so busted!"

"I wanted to give you these before you left," she said, handing me yet another *I Am Not a Plastic Bag* bag stuffed with papers.

"What's this?" I asked, sliding my hands through the green felt straps.

"Just a few articles I've clipped over the years," she explained. "They might help your project."

"That's right," I said, remembering my faux report. "Um, thanks. This is really helpful."

"If you'd like me to proof anything before you hand it in, just let me know."

Great. Now I was actually going to have to write the stupid fake paper. Like I didn't have enough real homework to do.

How, I wondered as I pulled the door shut behind me and padded across the front lawn, had I gotten here? How had I become the sort of person who lies to her mother so that she can sneak off with the captain of the lacrosse team?

Oh my god, I thought as a delicious thrill coursed through me. *I'm the sort of person who lies to her mom so that she can sneak off with the lacrosse captain!* I reached the end of my street and headed toward the meeting place I'd set up with Tanner. I'd told him I didn't want Kylie to see us together (which wasn't a lie, actually). But my mom would've freaked out.

I smiled. I couldn't help it. A month ago, the biggest lie I'd ever told my mother involved recycling bins and aluminum cans. (Why can't everything go into the same bag? Seriously. It just gets mashed up anyway.) And now here I was, sneaking off to meet the hottest guy in school.

Progress was progress. I was one of *those* girls. I was a glamazon minus the height and the glam. A perfect minus the perfection. I was a show on Disney. Or maybe ABC Family.

"In the mood for a party?" Tanner asked as I pulled open the car door.

"Sure." I slid in beside him, taking in his wet-from-the-shower blond hair and unfairly high cheekbones. He smelled good too. Deodorant mixed with some sort of cologne.

Tanner gunned the engine and the car lurched forward. I couldn't believe how calm I felt, considering this was my very first date and Tanner Mullins was, well, Tanner Mullins. Just the thought of attending Kylie's party had been enough to send me into a semipanic, but now here I was, completely relaxed. Even the angry red zit I'd spotted on my chin that morning couldn't sway me.

I leaned back against the seat and looked up at the starless black sky. A month ago it would have seemed creepy, but not tonight. Not now. I was popular. And popularity made everything shine.

TWENTY-THREE

"*L*ove your bag! Where'd you get it?"

I stood helplessly in the doorway as Jules lunged forward and grabbed the *I Am Not a Plastic Bag* bag, which, I suddenly realized, I'd forgotten to leave in Tanner's car.

"It's, um, you know, green," I said as she slipped her arms through the handles and checked out her reflection in the foyer's full-length mirror.

Jules blinked, either surprised I was pointing out something as obvious as the bag's color or wondering if Green was Marc Jacobs's new line.

"It's *sooo* cute," she cooed, recovering. "Is it from Barneys?"

I shook my head as Tanner's hand wrapped around mine. A thrill shot through me, followed quickly by a grimace as his fingers tightened. And tightened.

Ow.

I took a deep breath and silently repeated a "no pain, no gain" mantra as we walked together into the house, a big gray Colonial. It was owned by one of Tanner's jock friends, a football player named Chuck Todd, whose wide, squat body and lust for bench-pressing made him look more refrigerator than person.

Until the Skin, my only experience with Chuck had been indirect, through Gwen. On our third day of freshman year, he'd invented her nickname, Pot Roast Connolly. Now, as I watched him pull a can of dip out of his pocket and burp, I realized that, coming from him, the term was almost clever.

The place was packed, but as soon as we walked in, all attention had drifted our way. A tiny circle of lacrosse players and pep squad pepsters quickly pooled around, moving with us as we stepped farther into the house.

"I'm so glad you're here," Gina confided in my left ear. She'd grabbed the green bag from Jules and was now peering inside, inspecting its contents. "Jules has been driving me *crazy*. She won't stop talking about Spring Fling, but it's like, hello! *I'm* cochair."

"I need a beer," Tanner announced to no one in particular. His hand released my sore fingers as he turned and pushed his face into mine.

And then he kissed me. Just like that. It was quick, rough and, to be honest, a little wet. Hardly the innocent-yet-fiery first kiss I'd hoped for.

Still, my pulse kicked up a notch. Me. Tanner Mullins was kissing *me.*

He pulled back and turned away. "Where's the keg?"

"He's so cute," Jules whispered to me as the circle of jocks swept Tanner toward the kitchen and, I assumed, beer.

"He is," I murmured, though for some reason the words felt a little hollow. Was it rude that Tanner had just stolen a kiss, then walked away? He hadn't even offered to get me a beer. Not that I wanted one—the house already smelled and the floor felt sticky. It was sort of a turnoff. Besides, the Skin felt tighter tonight than it had during the day, and I was pretty sure that consuming much of anything would only make things worse.

But wasn't that the sort of thing that happened on dates? Guys got drinks, held open doors and placed their coats over mud puddles to protect their dates' footwear.

Let it go, I told myself. *He's Tanner Mullins.*

"You guys make a great couple too," Jules assured me. "Way better than Tanner and Kylie." She toyed with a long, stiff curl. "I have *no* idea what he even saw there in the first place."

I stared at her, wondering if she really and truly didn't remember more than a year's worth of Kylie-focused suck-up conversations.

I remembered. Every single one. Word for word.

"Whatever," Jules continued, glancing around the room to check out the crowd. "At least he came to his senses."

I followed her gaze, absorbing the sea of mini-me's in the room. Over the past few days, a huge outbreak of curly hair had swept through Woodlawn, and almost every girl wore a variation of my own outfit or one I'd worn in the recent past. There were no-name jeans, thermal tops and several dozen loose, long-sleeved T-shirts. I should have charged Lands' End for the free promotion. Woodlawn was looking more and more like a fishermen's wharf each day.

I smiled to myself, waiting for the familiar thrill to curl my stomach.

Only it didn't come. Not this time.

Easy.

The word popped into my head before I had a chance to block it out. It was true, too. There was something about the situation—all of it—that was way too easy. I hadn't done anything. I hadn't said a thing. And here I was, front and center on Woodlawn's red carpet. A month ago, I was so far from the carpet I could barely make out its color; today I was practically a fiber. And while I definitely wasn't ready to abandon my post, there was something a little eerie about it.

I shifted my weight, searching for a comfortable position. The Skin had moved past the point of control top and was heading for iron girdle territory.

"Can I borrow this sometime?" Gina was asking me. Her arm curled protectively around the *I Am Not a Plastic Bag* bag, giving off the distinct impression that by "borrow" she meant "take" and "sometime" meant "right now."

"Sure," I said, smiling at her. "No problem."

"How sweet are you?" Gina said, then pushed on. "So listen, I wanted to talk to you about Spring Fling committee."

Okay, that worked. At the mention of Spring Fling—Woodlawn's social event of the year—any misgivings I had about my recently acquired social status flew out of my head like a Frisbee.

"Really," I said, trying not to sound too interested. "What about it?"

"Well, you know Kylie was the other cochair," Gina said, looping her arm through mine like we were about to take a stroll through a croquet-friendly esplanade. "But now that she's crazy, we have to let her go." She waved her hand through the air dismissively. "So that leaves an open spot. We all think you'd be perfect."

I nodded, feeling excited and guilty and then even guiltier because I was so excited. Maybe, I rationalized, Kylie Frank's situation had nothing to do with me. Maybe she was headed for a crack-up anyway. How could I really know? After all, I'd only had one or two real conversations with her.

You deserve this, whispered a little voice inside my head. I'd spent last year's Spring Fling watching Gwen break in her new Dutch oven, and this year I was cochair of the whole dance. *Me.* I'd get to plan the invitations, paint the posters and decorate the gym . . . and, more importantly, I'd be there. At Spring Fling. Maybe even with Tanner.

I frowned slightly. Where *was* he, anyway? It didn't take this long to get a beer. Even I knew that.

I walked through the living room toward the kitchen.

"*Classic!*" Chuck Todd screamed. He was standing at the kitchen door, peering out at the backyard. "Mull-man *rules.*"

"What's going on?" I asked, pushing my way through the crowd.

Will Graves, captain of the tennis team, turned to me. "Man's making history," he said, pointing at the window.

Tanner was squatting at the edge of Chuck's swimming pool, surrounded by plastic cups. His head was bent and at first I thought he was simply studying the water, trying to decide whether or not he wanted to dive in.

And then he puked into the water. His body convulsed, producing a gag so loud I could hear it through the glass.

The jocks around me hooted appreciatively.

"Dude!" Chuck shouted. "I gotta bronze that filter."

I thought about all the Saturday nights I'd spent wondering what the A-list was up to. Wondering about what went on at all their parties, all the post-game busts. Wondering how it would feel to be the sort of person who was included rather than overlooked.

Mystery solved, I told myself as I went to look for Jules to ask for a ride home.

TWENTY-FOUR

"Come on," Alex chided. We were sitting in a corner at independent study, huddled over my geometry book. "You know what an acute angle is."

I shook my head. Was it my imagination or was I getting dumber? I vaguely remembered some sort of acronym or play on words—a cute little angle, maybe? Some sort of quip that successfully branded the definition into every brain but mine. I stared down at my last geometry test. The paper was filled with so many angry red marks and slashes I was tempted to get it an Ace bandage.

I was way past mnemonics.

"You need to stop spacing out in class," Alex told me, his voice hard. I hadn't spoken to him or Gwen since that day in front of my locker. Whenever they passed me in the hall, I could feel their gazes drop to the floor in purposeful avoidance. If Alex hadn't officially signed up as my geometry tutor, I was pretty sure he would've skipped the session.

I scowled, annoyed he was holding such a grudge. "I pay attention," I insisted. "It doesn't help."

"Um, I hate to argue with you, but . . ." Alex trailed off as he flipped through the pages of my geometry book. They were covered with doodles.

"Drawing helps me focus," I said quickly.

"You have to study or you're gonna flunk," he said matter-of-factly and without a trace of warmth.

Study? When? After Gina's Spring Fling invite, a slew of others had followed. There was fall fashion show, prom, dance and knitting club (I didn't know how to dance or knit, but that didn't seem to matter). Not to mention all the phone calls, IMs and mani/pedis with Gina, Jules and the rest of the pep pack—as Gwen sometimes called them. I was overbooked, overscheduled and completely exhausted. I had no time for geometry, which was why I'd been copying from Jules, who, it turned out, was even more of a math moron than I was.

"Just spend a good two hours every day working on this stuff," Alex said as the bell rang. "I'd start today if I were you."

I sighed. "I'm not sure I'll have time. I have a meeting after school. I think this one's about decorations." I frowned, trying to remember. "For something."

"Fine. Then tomorrow."

I shook my head. "Tanner has a game."

Alex snorted. "Well, that's definitely more important," he said, his voice heavy with sarcasm. "Why are you doing this, Sam?"

I clicked my mechanical pencil until the lead was about three inches long. "Doing what?"

"Changing," Alex said, shaking his head. "I just don't get it. It's like you've gone totally crazy."

"I'm just trying new things," I told him. "What's wrong with that? You've got your telescope and soapbox cars. Gwen cooks." I looked at him. "How about me? What do I do?"

Alex rubbed his chin thoughtfully. "For starters, you drink Snapple with a straw," he said, tilting his head toward my lemonade. "You read."

"I don't think *People* really counts."

"You study everyone around you," he continued. "And you draw." He looked up at me, his dark eyes wide. "Look, Sam, maybe the things you're interested in aren't that . . ." He frowned, searching for the right word. "*Formed.* But so what?" He tapped a doodle of my geometry teacher, Mr. Slater, getting beaten up by SpongeBob. "You're good at all of them."

I felt my shoulders lift. I missed Alex, I realized suddenly. I missed hanging out with him. As the second bell rang, I found myself wishing my afternoon were clear. I could go watch him work on one of his cars or something, just like before. If only I had time.

It's probably just as well, I thought as I started to pack my things. Tanner didn't seem like the sort of guy who'd ascribe to the whole guys-and-girls-can-be-friends theory.

Tanner Mullins.

Even after a week and a half of coupledom, the four syllables still sent little shivers up and down my spine. Every once in a while, from out of nowhere, his name would flash through my head like an alarm, followed by the thought: *I can't believe he likes me. . . .*

★ ★ ★

The day after Chuck's party, Tanner had shown up at my house and apologized. Sort of. "It happens," he'd explained. "When my boys and me get together, things can get a little out of hand."

Okay, so maybe it wasn't an apology. At all. But he'd sworn he wanted to spend the day with me, as a makeup for the night before. We'd driven out to the beach, and even though it was February—way too cold to swim—I was sort of looking forward to the trip. I pictured us skipping stones, building a bonfire. A repeat of my day with Alex, except with kissing.

As soon as we got to the beach, though, Tanner stripped off his shirt and stretched out on the sand.

"Aren't you freezing?" I asked, trying hard not to stare at the neat row of muscles that lined his abs. Even in the hard winter light, the skin on his chest looked smooth and toned.

He shrugged. "I want to build up a base before June," he explained. "That's when the serious sun hits." He tilted his chin up to the sky. "Listen, can you do something for me?"

"Sure, anything." *Here it comes,* I thought. *He's going to ask me to Spring Fling.*

"Can you time me?" he asked.

I blinked. "Time you?"

Tanner nodded. "I want to do ten minutes on each side." He glanced down at his perfect torso, as if that explained everything. "You know, so I don't get lines." He pointed at my watch, his face darkening with concern. "You do have a second hand on there, right?"

"Uh, sure," I told him. "Don't worry. Ten minutes."

"Nice. You're the best."

I watched as Tanner turned away from me and flipped open the latest issue of *Maxim*. I considered reading the *Cosmo* I'd stuck in my bag, but after one glance at the ocean, I closed my eyes and dove headfirst into the memory of my quarter birthday. Alex and I had collected seashells on this very same stretch of beach, just a few yards away. I giggled, remembering his bright green face.

"Hey, babe?" Tanner asked, glancing up from an article entitled "The Best Badass Movie Weapons." "You're still timing me, right? I mean, I just don't want you to break your concentration or anything. It's, like, my tan has to be even, you know?"

"Eight minutes left," I assured him.

He leaned over and gave me a quick, rough peck, then settled back into the sand and closed his eyes.

Yeah, the guy was a little vain. And his kisses were hardly the mind-blowing affairs I'd dreamed of. Still, he was an all-star lacrosse player and Woodlawn god. Plus, he was too hot for words.

It wasn't that my ultimate was less than ultimate. Real Tanner was just a little different from dream Tanner. A tiny bit of disappointment, I reasoned, was only natural. Expected, even.

Besides, the most important thing was that he liked *me*. Enough to ask me to Spring Fling on the drive home. We were a couple. *The* couple. And that was amazing.

I swung my backpack over my shoulder and followed Alex out of the room.

"See you next session," Alex said coolly, moving past me down the hall. He didn't wave or look back. Not once.

For a few seconds, I considered going after him.

You don't need to, chirped a little voice inside my head. *You have everything you want.*

It was true, too. For the new Sam Klein, the halls of Woodlawn High were lined with low-hanging fruit.

I was definitely in season.

TWENTY-FIVE

"9 think it's a *tragedy* that this school won't give us money for refreshments," Gina announced, with maximum drama. She shot an accusing glare around the table, as if each member of the Spring Fling planning committee was personally responsible for what was shaping up to be a pretzel-free evening.

"Seriously," Jules said, nodding emphatically. "What does that tell us about Woodlawn?"

Absolutely nothing? I thought as I pushed my face into what I hoped was a look of serious outrage. I glanced down at my watch. How was it possible that only twenty minutes had gone by?

"Isn't there *any* money left over for food?" Heidi asked, looking up from her knitting.

Gina opened her green *I Am Not a Plastic Bag* bag and pulled out the black bankbook where we logged our expenses. She flipped through a few pages and frowned. "We spent it all on the DJ."

I stifled a yawn and forced myself to pay attention. Ever since I was a freshman, I'd invested hours—entire days, even—fantasizing about events like Spring Fling and fall fashion show. But I'd never actually wondered how they came to be or what sort of planning was involved.

Well, now I knew.

The committees worked hard. Really hard. And at incredibly boring things. Like deciding which brand of poster board was the most cost-effective and which cleanup crew would be the most reliable.

And they took everything so seriously, too. That was the most amazing part about it. Every glue stick purchased represented a heated twenty-five-minute debate. The theme selection alone had practically resulted in a shoot-out between those in favor of "A Space Odyssey" and those who believed "Love Is All You Need" (after a bloody battle, space kicked love's butt).

It wasn't that I didn't want to go to the dance. I did. I'd even bought my dress—a black mini with a scoop neck and buttons down the back—along with my first pair of real stilettos (they were cloth, not leather, so I figured my mother would only throw a half fit). It was the sort of ensemble that just a few months ago had seemed off-limits but now I felt completely entitled to.

But I just couldn't seem to match the rest of the committee's enthusiasm for tissue paper and disco balls.

"I guess we'll just have to hold off on the refreshments for now," Gina said, the same way another person would say "I have six weeks to live." She sighed forlornly and glanced down at her clipboard. "Okay," she said, shaking off her despair. "Moving on. Decorations. Any ideas?"

"Pastels?" Adrienne suggested.

"Too girly," Heidi said, waving a knitting needle. "Besides, the theme's *space.*"

Adrienne wrinkled her nose. She'd lobbied heavily for love and was obviously still feeling bitter.

"Glitter," I blurted out, surprising myself. Color rushed to my cheeks as the heads around the table swiveled in my direction. "It's just, well, since the theme is space maybe we could cut the solar system out of cardboard and cover everything in glitter or even buy those glow-in-the-dark stars. . . ." I gulped, absorbing the stares and painful silence. "Or not," I finished weakly.

Gina flashed me a smile. "Fantastic," she declared as the room erupted into the sort of appreciative murmurs and congratulatory remarks usually reserved for Academy Award winners. "Just great."

"Really," breathed Jules, as if I'd just handed her a lifetime supply of Garnier. "I can't believe we didn't think of that."

Hmmm . . .

I shifted in my chair, trying hard to appreciate the praise and accept it all at face value. But it was sort of tough. I knew my idea was cute, but it was hardly Nobel Prize–worthy. It wasn't even particularly original. If I hadn't suggested it, I was pretty sure someone else would have.

I rubbed the Skin through the sleeve of my sweater. Was that all this was? If I stepped into the bathroom and slipped the Skin off (assuming I could—this morning it took me almost a half hour to wriggle out of it), would I return as invisible as I'd been this time last year? Was all the worship triggered by the stolen Skin?

You could put it to the test, murmured an incredibly unwelcome—and extremely annoying—voice in my head. *You could remove the Skin and see where that leaves you.*

So I did.

Abruptly, I stood and walked out of the room. When I reached the bathroom, I locked myself into the first stall, ripped the Skin from my body (literally—at this point, the Skin put superglue to shame) and stuffed it into my backpack. Then I took my plain old one-skinned self out for a test drive.

I made it about halfway down the hall. That was when the panic set in. I remembered the A-list's snooty disregard for the pre-Skin me. All those nights babysitting, channel surfing and wondering when my life was actually going to happen. What if I had to go back to that? I couldn't deal. I wasn't ready.

I needed the Skin.

I ran back to the bathroom and slipped it back on, relieved as it poured over my body. I headed back to the meeting, not minding the Skin's supersqueeze.

"Are you okay?" Gina asked as I pulled in my chair. "You ran out of here so fast. We were worried."

"Yeah, I, uh, just realized I forgot to say goodbye to Tanner. I wanted to catch him before he left."

Jules smiled teasingly. "It's so cute how you guys are so in love."

I leaned back. Maybe I was being too hard on myself before. Maybe my idea wasn't as generic as I'd thought. Maybe nobody else knew about glow-in-the-dark stars. . . .

"So, I guess that settles it," Gina said. "Thanks to Sam's brilliance, we've got the decorations all figured out."

"So that just leaves refreshments, right?" Heidi asked, unwinding some more yarn.

Gina frowned. "It's a real problem. After all our other expenses, we have less than fifty dollars to spend on food—and we need enough for the entire school."

"I know someone who might be able to help," I said, surprising myself again. Okay, so maybe my decorations idea wasn't all that groundbreaking. But this was pure genius.

"Really?" Gina asked. "Who?"

"I'll go talk to her now," I said, ignoring the question and leaving out the not-so-minor detail that the person I had in mind for the job was no longer speaking to me.

"Uh, great," Gina said as I grabbed my bag and raced out the door.

"Want some company?" Jules called after me, her voice hopeful. "I'll come with."

But it was too late. I was already gone.

★　★　★

The plan was simple, I decided as I tore through the mall fifteen minutes later. All I had to do was get Gwen to stop hating me and agree to cater Spring Fling for free. It was a tall order, definitely, but not completely impossible.

When I'd called Gwen, her mom had told me that she was at Williams-Sonoma. I found her standing in front of the Le Creuset display, testing the weight of a blue frying pan. "Oh!" she said sweetly as I plowed down the aisle. "If it isn't Woodlawn High's celebutard of the moment."

Okay, I was dead. Beyond dead. I was puree.

"I'm really sorry about everything," I gushed, struggling to catch my breath. (All those torturous pep squad practices and I still couldn't run through a shopping center? How was that even possible?) "I wanted to call you and straighten things out but I—"

"Forget it," she said, cutting me off with a snort. I took an involuntary step backward. There was something a little menacing about the way she was shifting the pan from one hand to the other. "I'm the one who should be apologizing." She looked at me, her eyes stormy. "I'm sure your high-gloss, highlighted friends are pining away for you at this very moment."

"Listen," I said, suddenly exhausted. "I'm really sorry. I know I've been unreliable and

I'm sorry if I've been so out of touch. But you know, you and Alex are the ones who stopped talking to *me*."

Gwen flipped the frying pan over to check the price, sighed and dropped it back on to the table. "Please. Don't even try to blame-shift. You're guilty of blow-off." She paused, considering. "In the first degree."

Clearly, this wasn't working. I needed another tack.

"Look," I said slowly as Gwen flipped open a book entitled *Tarts for a Tart*. "I'm sorry I messed up, but I'm here now. And I actually wanted to talk to you about something."

"I wonder if I could replace Grand Marnier with Cointreau," Gwen mused loudly, head bent over a recipe entitled, "Tart and Tipsy!" "I really have to get my hands on a fake ID so I can start buying liqueur."

"Well, um, next weekend's Spring Fling and, you know, I'm on the planning committee." Ignoring Gwen's disdainful eye roll, I pushed on. "We're having a little trouble deciding what to do about refreshments, since we want them to be really good." I took a deep breath and did my best to ignore the "Liar, Liar, Pants on Fire" chant that was now blasting through my head. "So I mentioned your name."

Gwen gaped at me. "Me? Why?"

"I thought you might want to cater."

"What do you mean cater?" she asked, clapping the book shut. "All you need is a few bags of cheese curls and some punch and you're good to go."

"Not if you take the job," I persisted. "You could serve anything you wanted. Meringues. Biscotti. Eight different kinds of brownies. Go crazy."

"I don't think so," Gwen said, narrowing her eyes, which, I noticed, had started to shine with interest. "You know I never set foot in Woodlawn outside of mandatory school hours."

"Okay," I said, thinking fast. "Then treat it as a job, not a social event. You'll be working."

"I do need to break in my new ramekins," Gwen murmured, eyeing the tart book longingly.

"Great," I encouraged heartily, even though I was pretty sure I wouldn't know a ramekin if one bit me. "The committee can't pay a lot, but—"

"I can't scrimp on quality," Gwen cut in. "But the manager at Marvelous Markets gives me a frequent-shopper discount. Besides, I wouldn't be doing this for the money." She paused, then added: "If I do this."

"Definitely."

Gwen leaned back against the bookshelf and folded her arms across her chest. "Fine," she announced loudly. "But I have some terms."

Oh my. "Anything," I said, plastering an ac-commodating smile on my face.

"*I'm* in charge of the menu, not Jules or Gina or anyone else." She sniffed loudly. "If I see a single Dorito or Frito—or any other sort of ito—I quit."

"Got it. You're in charge."

"And no cheesy pop music."

I looked at her. "Um, I think that might be sort of hard," I said. "It's a high school dance."

Gwen sighed. "Fine. Then how about nothing in the top ten?"

I shook my head.

"Come on," Gwen pleaded. "I can handle top twenty, but anything under ten makes me gag."

"Fine," I said. "I'll see what I can do."

Gwen grabbed the tart book and started flipping through the pages. The touch alone seemed to trigger a contact high. Her cheeks were flushed, her dark eyes wide and shining. "I think I'll make something with pears," she muttered. "And maybe almonds."

You did it, I thought, resisting the urge to give myself a brief round of applause. I'd found a way to set things right with Gwen *and* prove that she had a place in my new-and-improved life. And I'd solved Spring Fling's refreshment woes, too. The pep pack was going to love me. Even more.

"Are clementines still in season?" Gwen wondered aloud. She pushed her face so close to the cookbook she was practically making out with the page.

Should I feel guilty about this? I wondered. Gwen was obviously thrilled at the prospect of her very first catering gig, but did the fact that she was also solving a problem for me—and didn't even know it—mean that I was using her?

At this point it was sort of hard to tell. I sighed and reached into my bag to grab my cell phone. It was, of course, ringing.

TWENTY-SIX

Forty minutes. I had forty minutes to get home, change, write a paper on the New Deal and study for a biology quiz. Then I had to head back to school to catch the rest of the lacrosse game and brainstorm fund-raising ideas for pep squad.

Plus, I had nineteen new voice mails.

Nineteen.

If I didn't start callbacks now, the number would double by the end of the day. I'd be up all night wading through messages. Plus, there was the geometry situation to deal with. I'd probably end up copying Jules's work. Again. And even though cheating off her was both crime and punishment rolled up in one, it was still cheating.

But what choice did I have? There just wasn't enough time.

I glanced at my watch and tried to pick up my pace. Gina had offered me a ride but I'd turned her down. I'd been in the mood to walk. Or maybe it was that I wanted to be alone, I realized now as I stepped into a huge puddle of gray slush. Lately, whenever I moved, I was either on my cell or with an entourage—always answering, responding or reacting. It felt nice not to do that.

I looked up and found myself staring at a sign featuring two ultrasmiley men with entirely too much hair. Ben and Jerry. Even though it was freezing outside, I was tempted to order a cone. I'd skipped lunch for knitting club and hadn't eaten a thing all day.

Through the window, I perused the list of flavors, then remembered my abbreviated pep squad uniform. It showed every roll, pad and bulge. On the other hand, it didn't seem to matter. And I was already late. Why not indulge?

I placed my hand on the door, then froze when I saw the store's only two customers.

Ella and Kylie were sitting on the black stools that lined the counter. A huge bowl of ice cream rested between them, smothered in brownie chunks, whipped cream and pretty much every other topping imaginable. I narrowed my eyes, focusing on Kylie. I hadn't really thought about her since the pep squad meltdown a few weeks back. After a few days, the talk around school had faded and even though I saw her every morning in homeroom, she and Ella kept to themselves. I barely noticed Kylie Frank anymore.

Inside the store, Ella's lips moved and Kylie threw her head back and laughed. She wasn't wearing any makeup and her hair was pulled into a messy ponytail that swung back and forth, skimming her gray sweatshirt. Unlike her first days without the Skin, her cheeks were flushed with pink and her face was smooth and worry-free. She looked fresh, as if she'd just stepped off the set of an Ivory soap commercial. And she looked happy. She looked, I realized with the first stab of envy I'd felt since donning the Skin, better than ever.

Now both Kylie and Ella were laughing. Actually, laughing was an understatement. They were borderline hysterical, clutching their stomachs and convulsing. Their mirth was so intense I could push my face up against the glass for a better look without even worrying they'd see me.

I tried to remember the last time I'd had an afternoon like that. No meetings. No practice. No pressure. Just hanging out and getting silly. I couldn't pretend it had ever happened with Jules or Gina. The closest I'd come to hysterics with them, or any other member of the pep pack, was when I'd tried to do a split and couldn't get up. Nope, nothing like the persimmon-square afternoon at Gwen's house had happened with my new friends.

Okay, enough, I told myself, backing away from the door. *What are you even thinking? You ruined Kylie's life and you're still jealous of her? You're a nightmare. Get over it.*

I turned roughly away and trudged down the street. Sure, Kylie Frank had time to relax. What else did she have to do? Her rung had dropped considerably on the popularity ladder. Mine, on the other hand, was shiny and polished. Numero uno. My life was perfect. I had no reason to complain, because, really, I could do whatever I wanted.

So long as popularity gave me the go-ahead.

TWENTY-SEVEN

"9 think Jupiter looks sort of crooked," Adrienne announced, frowning up at me as I stood on the stepladder desperately trying to balance a jumbo roll of masking tape, a cardboard planet and myself.

"Wait," I said, teetering slightly. "Is it droopy or just tilted? Because it's supposed to be tilted. All the planets are on an axis."

"God, how do you even know that?" Jules said proudly, as if I were her kid and had just made the honor roll.

I shrugged, sending a silent thank-you to

Alex. If it weren't for him, my knowledge of space would still be limited to the occasional bowl of Lucky Charms and TBS airings of *Star Wars*. Our geometry tutorials were still tense, but last session I'd managed to convince him to blow off the Pythagorean theorem and give me a crash course in astronomy. It had taken the entire period—easily twice the amount of time a normal, science-friendly brain would've needed—for the information to soak in. And while I was still no Carl Sagan, I'd walked away armed with enough information about orbits, planets and moons to transform the Woodlawn High cafeteria into a galaxy far, far away.

"I still think it looks weird," Adrienne said. Her eyes skipped to my face and she added a hasty, "But if you think it's fine I'm sure it is."

I climbed down from the ladder and looked around the room. Not bad. Not too bad. Sure, the Little Dipper was upside down, and the black circle hanging from the ceiling looked more black eye than black hole. But all in all, the place was really shaping up. Nice and spacey. And we were just about done.

It was a good thing too. After almost a solid week of decorating, my hands were covered in paint. I could do just about anything with a glue gun, and I was pretty sure I'd be washing glitter out of my hair, and lord knows where else, until graduation. Plus, I was exhausted. And the dance was less than five hours away.

I faked a yawn and tried to lift my arms above my head. I got about as high as my shoulders before I flinched. The Skin was holding me back. When I'd woken up that morning, it felt tighter than ever. Like I was wearing a child's wet suit.

"Oh!" Jules squealed, bending and stretching alongside me. "Pre-dance calorie burner!" She tilted her head toward me knowingly. "My dress is so tight if I eat even one Twizzler I won't be able to zip it up."

You don't know the half of it, I thought, clasping my hands behind my back. I tried to raise them but they refused to budge any higher than my hips. I frowned. I was never the most flexible person in the world—pep squad had certainly proven that point—but this was ridiculous.

The rest of the pep pack circled round me and immediately began twisting their bodies into a series of gravity-defying shapes.

"This is such a great idea," Adrienne added, a look of pure glee on her face as she kicked her leg up, touching her knee to her head. "I didn't have time to work out this morning!"

Resisting the urge to zap her with the glue gun, I tried to force my body into a single jumping jack. I was barely halfway through when my cell rang.

Thank you, I thought as I flipped it open.

"Yo," Tanner said. I'd realized weeks ago that normal pleasantries—like "please," "goodbye" and "sorry I just pounded you on the back when a simple pat would do"—weren't his style. "I'm still at the game."

"Game?" I asked, my mind a complete blank. "You're at a game now?"

"Yeah, you know. Up at Valley." He sounded surprised that I'd forgotten. And a little annoyed. "Looks like my boys and I have an overtime situation on our hands. Could be a few more hours. Better hit the dance without me, okay?"

"What do you mean? We were supposed to go together."

"Sorry, babe," Tanner said, not sounding very sorry at all. "But duty calls. Gotta go. This photographer's snapping my pic and I want to make sure he gets my name in the caption. . . . Hey, man, that's Tanner with two ns, okay?"

"But—" I sputtered as the phone clicked off.

Great. I, Samantha Klein, the most popular girl at Woodlawn High and cochair of the Spring Fling committee, was minus one dream date.

"What's wrong?" Jules asked, noticing the look of alarm on my face. "Did you forget to buy something?" She patted my arm reassuringly. "Don't worry about it. I've got extras of everything."

I had to get out of here.

"Uh, listen," I said, backing away from the group. "The paint fumes are giving me a headache. I'm gonna take a walk."

I shot out of the room, ignoring Jules's predictable "Wait! I'll come with!"

Not good. This is so not good, I thought as I pushed open the blue fireproof doors that led to the parking lot. I *had* to go to Spring Fling. It was *my* dance—*my* night. Everyone knew I was a shoo-in for Spring Fling Queen. How could I not show? Of course, Jules would definitely let me tag along with her and Chuck—but that was so lame. So old me.

Nope. I definitely needed an escort. Only all the guys were taken . . .

Except one.

The idea fluttered through my head like the Albert Einstein of butterflies. I flipped open my cell and punched in Alex's number.

He picked up almost immediately.

Thank you for having absolutely no social life, I thought. "Hey!" I began, cheerfully. "What are you doing right now?"

"Sam?" Alex asked. He sounded surprised and not particularly pleased. "Is that you?"

"Duh! Of course it's me, silly," I said. Wait—was that my voice? It sounded thicker than usual, with a definite flirty undertone. "What are you up to?"

"Uh, I was just heading out to the roof," Alex said. I could picture him, standing in the middle of his room wearing a stained T-shirt and pants that were baggy in a way that never had been—and never would be—fashionable. "Remember the lunar phases I told you about? Well, tonight's the waxing gibbous."

"Sounds great," I lied, thinking that a waxing gibbous sounded more like a wrestling move than a moon cycle. "But I was wondering if you wanted to go to Spring Fling."

There was silence on the other end of the line.

"Wait, with you?" Alex said, after a few more painful seconds had slipped by.

Okay, not exactly the enthusiastic response I was looking for, but not necessarily a no.

I giggled. "Yes with me."

"But I thought Tanner was taking you," Alex said, his tone icy. This too was easy to picture. His eyes were narrowed, his jaw set. I'd go with clenched fists and white knuckles, too.

Alex definitely had a jock complex.

My heart twisted. If I told the truth—that he was no more than a last-minute sub—I'd hurt his

215

feelings *and* be dateless. It was a lose-lose all around.

"Look, I know things have been sort of weird between us lately, so I thought maybe we could hang out tonight." I squeezed my eyes shut as I threw myself into yet another lie. "Besides, I decided I'd rather go to the dance with someone I'm really comfortable with. Someone like you."

Another silence. Was I imagining things or did this one feel different from the first? Less tense.

"Uh, what time should I pick you up?" Alex asked. His voice was warmer now, almost happy.

Whew. As much as it could, my body relaxed under the iron grip of the Skin. "How 'bout eight?" I suggested.

"Great," he said. "And listen, Sam?"

"Yeah?"

"Thanks."

"We're gonna have fun," I said, hanging up the phone.

Crisis averted, I thought as I turned onto my street. I tried to imagine the night ahead but it was hard. I'd spent so long dreaming about Spring Fling with Tanner—dancing with Tanner, laughing with Tanner, kissing Tanner (*real* kisses this time—not the hasty pecks from past dates). Now my brain had less than three hours to revise the picture with Alex instead. There would definitely be laughing. But what about dancing? Doubtful. And kissing was out of the question.

Me. Kissing Alex.

I waited for a knot to form in my stomach. Or nausea. Or some other vile physical response. Nothing happened. My pulse fluttered a little, but I was pretty sure that was due to the walking, not the kissing.

Whatever, I thought, climbing the steps to my room. I tried to raise my knees extra high to give the Skin a good stretch. At least I had a date.

I slipped out of my clothes and ran a bath. And then I tried to slide the Skin off of my body.

Only I couldn't. It was completely and totally stuck.

I pulled. And tugged. And hopped. Nada. The Skin clung to me like melted plastic. I spent the next forty minutes trying to get it off, with absolutely no results.

Sore and exhausted, I looked at the clock. Alex would be over in less than a half hour and I was still sweaty and paint-covered. In a panic, I hopped into the tub and prayed that the Skin wouldn't melt like the Wicked Witch of the West.

Lather. Rinse. Repeat. No damage done. And as I stepped out of the tub, the Skin dried almost immediately. I barely needed a towel.

As clean as a laminated body can get, I put on

my dress and shoved my feet into my new stilettos, then stomped around my room trying to scuff
the soles.

Calm down, I ordered. *Don't think about the
Skin. You don't have time.*

Spring Fling was about to be flung.

TWENTY-EIGHT

"**N**ot bad," Alex said, looking around the cafeteria. The Little Dipper, I noticed, was still upside down, but Alex was kind enough to overlook that point. "I'd have included at least one *Star Trek* reference, but other than that I'm impressed." He turned to me, his hand extended. "Congratulations. I'm sure you'll get into space camp."

"Thanks," I said, flashing him a weak smile as we walked past Saturn. From the main room to the ministage, the place was packed, covered with constellations and filled with music. Spring Fling was a success.

And I was freaking out.

This wasn't just post-traumatic guilt from the many white—okay, beige—lies I'd spewed either. And it had nothing to do with all the glitter I'd inhaled over the past week or the fact that I was now permanently shrink-wrapped (although yes, that was definitely freaky).

The main reason for my current weird-out had to do with Alex. Yes, Alex. My geeky-but-hilarious, known-him-since-just-about-forever friend Alex.

I'd actually been doing pretty well, considering. As I'd stood in the foyer waiting for him to pick me up, I kept offering myself words of silent encouragement—*you can do it!* and *keep it up!*—sort of like I was my own personal trainer.

And then the bell rang.

Alex was standing in the doorway, hair freshly washed and cut, wearing a suit. He looked so normal. And so *tall.* And so incredibly . . . *wow.*

My heart did an Olympic-caliber double axel inside my chest. I'd never felt anything like it before. Not with Tanner. Not with anyone in *People* magazine's "Top Ten Hottest Bachelors" issue. Not with anyone on a billboard.

And definitely not with Alex.

The excitement was totally weird, and completely unwelcome (as were the admiring glances I'd seen several girls cast his way since we'd walked in; I almost kicked them). I had way too much going on already. I just couldn't handle this.

Besides, I had a boyfriend. His name was Tanner Mullins and he was perfect. Okay, perfect-looking. Whatever. The point was, I didn't need any more complications. Not now. Now was Spring Fling. I'd waded through weeks of boring meetings and a sea of arts and crafts supplies just to get here. It was my night. And it was supposed to be easy and problem-free.

"You look amazing," Jules said, approaching.

How'd she do it? I wondered, staring at her dress. I'd been completely close-mouthed about my Spring Fling fashion choices. I'd shopped alone and kept the whole ensemble hidden in the back of my closet for weeks. But somehow Jules had managed to outfit-stalk me anyway. Her dress was a variation of my own—black mini verging on micro, buttons down the back—and she was wearing the exact same pair of Steve Madden heels.

I glanced around. With all the curly hair in the room, the cafeteria was screaming for a huge squirt of Frizz-Ease. And almost every girl was wearing a minidress, too. It was like a sixties tribute fest.

Oh, let it go, I thought, turning to Jules. "Thanks," I said. "You look great too. Nice dress."

She smiled, completely unaware that by complimenting her I was basically complimenting myself.

"Hi, Alan," she said, noticing Alex for the first time.

"Hey," he said coolly. He turned to me. "Um, listen, Sam. Can I talk to you for a second? Alone?"

Oh my. This wasn't going to work. How could I have a vapid, thought-free evening with Alex around making my pulse do all the extreme pep squad–style moves my body refused to even attempt?

"Sure," I said, thinking fast. "But could you do me a huge favor first? I'd love a Diet Coke."

Alex tilted his head to one side. "A Diet Coke," he repeated.

"Right. Extra cold."

He shrugged. "Uh, sure. Be right back."

It wasn't a nice thing to do, I thought as I watched him disappear into the throng. But compared to the other not-nice things I'd done in the past few weeks, it barely hit the top ten.

Not that that made me feel any better.

"Congrats on the refreshments," Heidi said, walking up to me. She also wore a minidress, which struggled to cover her long, thin body. She lifted a plate of pastries. "Have you tried the mini éclairs? They're amazing."

Uh-oh, I thought, swinging my head toward the refreshments table. I'd completely forgotten that Gwen was cooking. And that Gwen was at the dance.

Judging from the look she was shooting my way, the slight hadn't gone unnoticed. Since the scene in Williams-Sonoma, we were no longer in an official fight. But I was definitely on probation.

"Be right back," I told Jules and Heidi, and cut across the room.

Ouch. The Skin was seriously digging into my side. I felt like I was being liposuctioned.

"Thanks so much for leaving the chick clique behind," Gwen said as I approached. "Very considerate. It's dangerous to have all that hair product near the food."

"Wow," I said, looking down at the table. It was covered with desserts: lemon squares, Linzer cookies, petit fours and brownies. They were all there, spread out on long silver trays. "Move over, Martha Stewart."

Gwen rolled her eyes. "Hack," she muttered under her breath. She looked at me, the hint of a smile on her lips. "It turned out pretty well, right? I was a little worried about the seven-layer bars but I think—"

I shook my head. "Everything looks great. Really. Thanks so much."

"No problem. It was actually sort of fun." She turned just as Chuck Todd plucked five meringues from the buffet and shoved them into his mouth at once.

I winced as Gwen's expression leapt from satisfied to offended.

Don't say anything, I begged silently. *Oh please don't say anything.*

Evidently, I was in no position to ask for favors.

Gwen stalked over to Chuck. "Can't you at least chew?" she demanded, waving her hand over the spread. "This stuff didn't exactly come from a *mix.*"

Chuck snorted. "What's the big deal, Pot Roast?" he asked, clearly amused. He swiped a few chocolate lace cookies from a tray. "I'll bet you pack away twice that much."

I watched, horrified, as laughter erupted around us. Gwen's cheeks colored and her mouth dropped open, ready to deliver the insult her brain hadn't yet formed.

I took a step toward Chuck, ready to tell him to shut up, when Gwen's eyes met mine.

"Oh my god," she breathed, incredulous. "You're smiling."

I was? No way. My hands flew to my mouth, touching the plastic grin that stretched across my face. *I was.*

A shiver ran down my spine. It was like I was

watching myself through the lens of a camera, from across the room. My head was tilted; my hair frizzed down the back of my slinky dress . . . and my mouth was frozen into a big, phony smile. It was me. Definitely me. But I was completely unrecognizable.

"I didn't mean—" I started in. God, her face was killing me. I could handle Gwen's sarcasm. I even expected it. But this—all the hurt and disappointment—it was too much.

"Who are you?" she asked, shaking her head. Tears swam in her eyes. "I mean, really?"

I had no idea. But before I had a chance to say anything, a song blasted through the speakers. I recognized it immediately as one of Jules's favorites. It was light, poppy . . . and definitely in the top ten.

Gwen tossed me a final, pained smile. "Perfect," she said, turning away. "Just perfect."

"See ya, Pot Roast!" Chuck Todd shouted after her as she disappeared through the crowd. His jock friends whooped appreciatively.

Shut up.

I thought the words, but for some reason couldn't say them. It didn't really matter anyway. I was too late.

"Hey," Alex said, appearing by my side, Diet Coke in hand. "I tried three different tables—this one's definitely the coldest."

"Uh, thanks," I said, grabbing the can. I had to find Gwen. I had to make things right between us or I'd never be able to live with myself.

"So listen," Alex said. "About before . . . I wanted to talk to you."

"Um, could we maybe do this later?" I asked, feeling extra clumsy. "Now's not really a good time—"

"The thing is: I'm in love with you."

"You . . ." I trailed off, unable to finish. My head was spinning as the planet-filled room fell away. *This is real,* I told myself. *This is really happening.*

"Right. I love you," Alex said, sounding relieved and not at all nervous. "I have for—well, pretty much for forever."

I stared at him as several different and completely contradictory reactions twisted inside me. On the one hand, I was too shocked to process much of anything and was in serious danger of hyperventilating. I felt like I'd just completed four back-to-back pep squad practices.

Another part of me heard the words but refused to believe them. I simply wasn't worthy. Alex was too good for me. Too smart. Too cute. Too honest. He was completely out of my league.

But at the same time—and I realize this makes absolutely no sense—I wasn't shaken at all.

Alex's "I've loved you forever" speech wrapped around me, as warm and comfortable as cashmere. It felt great and I was glad to hear it. Definitely.

Then, finally, came the ugly part—the awful part. The one that told me this simply wouldn't work. Samantha Klein and Alex Ashby? *Come on.* The most popular girl in school and a guy who builds soapbox cars? Impossible . . .

It was, without a doubt, the cruelest moment I'd ever had. I hated myself for thinking it. And I hated myself even more for believing it was true.

This was too much. Too intense. I needed an out.

"Mullins is here!"

"There *is* a god!"

I looked up to see Tanner, still dressed in full lacrosse garb, stomping across the floor. He was covered in mud and carrying a trophy easily half his size.

That's it, I thought as he lifted the trophy high above his head and started to belt a very out-of-tune and—thanks to the mouth guard he was still wearing—garbled rendition of "We Will Rock You." Tanner was the perfect escape hatch. If I was in love with him, I couldn't be in love with Alex. And that would mean all the racing-pulse, palpitating-heart nonsense from before was just, well, nonsense. I'd be completely off the hook! I wouldn't have to think about any of this stuff ever again.

Turning away from Alex, I smiled in Tanner's direction and clapped along with the rest of the cafeteria. (For the record, there was also a lot of hooting going on but I refrained.) It wasn't a nice thing to do. At all. But compared to what happened next, it was nothing.

This isn't so bad, I thought as Tanner caught my eye. He lurched forward, swept me into his arms—okay, it was more like a grab—and kissed me. Seriously kissed me. In front of the entire school.

Including Alex.

I knew it was a mistake almost instantly, as soon as his sweat-soaked face descended. His lips felt hard against mine and, despite the fact that he'd finally removed his mouth guard, there was a definite slobber situation happening. He smelled, too. Like grass and sweat and dirt—but not in a way that was manly or appealing. Just smelly.

My entire body locked. I squeezed my eyes shut and an image of Alex popped into my head. Or, to be precise: the image was of Alex and me. Together.

And that was when I relaxed and got into things. My resistance melted, my body welcomed and my lips searched for more.

Now *this* was a kiss.

"Tanner Mullins rules!"

The hoot yanked me back to reality. I opened my eyes. The real Alex was standing beside me. Watching his date make out with someone else.

I turned to him. "Wow, I'm—"

He held up his hand, cutting me off. His mouth was a thin, hard line across his face and his eyes were fierce.

"Don't," he said. "Just forget it."

And then, just as the cafeteria burst into a thunderous round of applause for Woodlawn's supercouple, he was gone.

I was alone. Stuck with Tanner Mullins and our overwhelming popularity.

TWENTY-NINE

What I really needed, I thought as I followed Tanner and Jules into the Spring Fling after-party at Chuck Todd's house, was a good case of amnesia.

I'd spent the remainder of the dance praying for something to hit me on the head—hard. A shooting star. Or better yet, a planet.

No such luck. Thanks to the Spring Fling committee's investment in extra-strength masking tape, those constellations weren't going anywhere. And that left me trapped at the dance, tormented by all the awful things I'd done. Somewhere along the line, the rewrite of my life had gone from bodice-ripping beach read to trashy horror story—the sort of thing I'd buy in the ninety-nine-cent bin at Walmart, if my parents let me shop there.

I'd messed up on so many different levels, with so many different people. I should have defended Gwen. I was *going* to. Okay, maybe my response was a little delayed, but I was, for the record, going to say something.

Alex was another story. I'd treated him terribly.

The thought made me want to cry.

To top it all off, Spring Fling—the dance I'd coveted my entire high school career—was quickly becoming the absolute worst night of my life.

After our kiss, Tanner and I were voted King and Queen. Surprise surprise. As we made our way up toward the stage to collect the crowns, the gym dissolved into a mess of howls and whistles, and Tanner hooted and hollered right back. The best I could muster was another superfake grin, which, considering the Skin was now king cobra-tight, required Lance Armstrong–style discipline.

Then I had to dance. With Tanner. All night. After one song, I was covered in sweat. By two, my dress was more mud than fabric. And I spent most of the third composing a nasty complaint to

Right Guard in my head, since Sport Stick in no way protects anyone from BO.

And I couldn't stop fiddling with the crown. Not only did it look like it had been fished out of a Happy Meal, clearly the thing hadn't been designed with curly hair in mind. No matter how hard I tugged, my frizz kept forcing it up into a jaunty angle that would've been perfect if I'd been wearing a beret—which, of course, I wasn't.

I can't believe I used to dream about this stuff, I thought, glancing around Chuck's living room. The whole A-list was there and, from the number of kegs being rolled into the kitchen, they were in the mood to do some serious drinking.

"Keystone?" Tanner said scornfully, eyeing a label. "Stuff tastes like weasel piss."

Jules giggled, which I'd learned was her standard "cute boy" response. Since I had no thoughts on, or interest in, the weasel's urinary tract, I opted for silence.

"Listen, grab me a cup, okay, babe?" Tanner said. Because of the "babe," I was pretty sure the request was meant for me, but it was hard to tell since he was already en route to the kitchen. "I'm gonna go help those boys with the tap." He shook his head forlornly. "They've got, like, no clue, you know?"

I watched him walk away, feeling nothing but relief.

I can't do it, I thought. *I can't spend another night watching Tanner and his buddies do keg laps, keg tosses and whatever else you can do with a keg.*

I had to get out of there.

"I think I'm gonna go," I told Jules.

She gaped at me. "But we just got here."

"I know, but I'm really tired." I faked a yawn. "The dance really wore me out."

"But what about Tanner?"

"He's a big boy. He can get his own cup."

Jules tried again. "But you're gonna miss *everything.*"

I shrugged. "I'll live."

"Okay," she said reluctantly. "I'll call you tomorrow and give you a full rundown."

Don't bother, I thought. *I don't want to know.*

It was true, I realized suddenly. I didn't care about missing the party. I didn't care about who said what and who hooked up with whom. I just wasn't interested.

"Thanks," I said as I pushed my way toward the front door. I considered telling Tanner I was leaving but decided to skip it. He was in the kitchen, surrounded by beer and jocks. He'd be fine. More than fine.

I stood on the street waiting for the car service I'd called, happy to be away from all the people and the noise. Just a few months ago, I'd have given anything to be inside. Now I felt just the opposite. I'd do anything—no sum was too much, no sacrifice too great—to avoid another A-list event.

Plus, the Skin was killing me. At this point, I was basically vacuum-sealed.

One thing was certain, I decided, as the car pulled up. I wasn't confused. Not anymore.

I'd had it. I wanted out. Out of the Skin. Out of pep squad. Out of my unrelationship with Tanner.

I wanted my life back. My real life.

I wanted Gwen and—with an intensity that was almost frightening—I wanted Alex.

I climbed out of the car, wondering if there was anything I could do, short of time travel, to get Gwen and Alex to forgive me.

And then, as if on cue, there they were. Standing on Kylie Frank's front porch. I watched, completely frozen, as Alex (*my* Alex) and Gwen (*my* Gwen) stood joking around with Kylie and Ella. They looked as if they'd been friends for years.

Jealousy descended, weaving its way through the Skin and into my pores. Obviously, this was some sort of setup. Kylie Frank's idea of revenge.

I'd stolen the Skin, so now she was stealing my friends. My real friends. She didn't like them. Not really. She was just trying to get to me.

Well, I thought as I watched the happy four-some issue their goodbyes. *Mission accomplished.*

I couldn't see straight. I wasn't thinking. I know that doesn't excuse what I did next, but please—just keep it in mind.

As Alex's car, with Gwen and Ella in it, backed out of the driveway, I felt myself hurtling toward the porch as fast as a body bound in synthetic skin could move.

"That's so low!" I yelled. I tried to storm up the stairs but, since bending my knees was sort of impossible, had to settle for a much less intimidating hop. "I can't believe you!"

Kylie's eyes widened with surprise, then, as she recovered, started to flash. "What are you talking about?" she snapped.

"Oh, like you don't know," I countered. "Look, I'm sorry things haven't been exactly going your way, but you don't have to use my friends to get back at me."

"What? We just ran into each other at—" She stopped midsentence and seemed to give herself a little shake. "You know what?" she hissed. "I don't have to explain myself to you. Get off my porch."

Despite my temporary insanity and the fact that the Skin was most definitely cutting off the oxygen supply to my brain, I could see she had a point.

I tossed a final poisonous look her way and started to hop back down the stairs. And that was when it hit. A thought so painful it made my heart hurt. "I suppose you and Alex are like a *thing* now, right?" I screamed. My voice was shrill and shaking. "Is that what this is all about? Punishment for Tanner?"

As soon as the words were out of my mouth, I knew I was wrong. And I also knew I'd gone too far.

Kylie flew in front of me. "How dare you! *You're* the one who runs around taking friends and boyfriends without even thinking about it!" Her face twisted with anger. "I never did anything to you except trust you with *one* secret, which you . . ."

She turned away from me and pulled open the door. "You know what? You're not worth it. Just forget it."

I watched as she stomped back inside the house. And that was when I snapped. I couldn't take it anymore. I wanted out.

"Okay!" I cried as I followed her. "You're right. I'm sorry!"

Kylie froze, then turned slowly around to face me. "For what?" she asked, her voice suspicious.

Even though I was dreading the scene about to unfold, there was a not-so-small part of me that also felt pretty good. Okay, maybe good was a stretch. But I did feel sort of calm. I wanted this to be over. All of it. I was ready.

I took a deep breath and did something I hadn't done in ages.

I told the truth.

THIRTY

"*W*hy did you tell me this now?" Kylie asked, after I'd confessed. We were standing in the middle of her living room, in front of the repaired picture window. We stared at each other from opposite ends of the room.

I started to cry. Fat, sloppy tears rolled down my face and into my mouth. "I don't want the Skin anymore," I sputtered. "You can have it. I just want it off."

Kylie looked at me. "Why? What are you talking about?"

"I'm sorry. I wasn't trying to mess up your life." The words rushed out as if spurting from a showerhead. "Really. I actually sort of wor-shiped you. Okay, not sort of. I did. I wanted to *be* you."

Kylie folded her arms protectively across her chest. "And you thought the best way to be me was to steal the Skin and ruin my life," she said. "Because you did ruin my life. You know that, right?"

I nodded. "I didn't mean to. That part just sort of . . . happened. I just wanted to be popular. I was obsessed." I wiped at my eyes with the back of my hand. "But not anymore. I mean it. I want to be myself again. . . ." I trailed off, wondering who, exactly, that was.

Kylie looked at me, her face inscrutable. "So take it off and give it back."

"I've tried," I said, sniffling loudly. "I can't. It's stuck." I reached through the sleeve of my dress and pulled at the Skin. "I . . . Look . . . that day in your room you said something about a list of rules and a user's manual. . . . If you could just—"

Kylie snorted. "Please. Why would I even *consider* helping you?"

"I know," I said. "But how about this. If you help me, you can have the Skin back. Seriously. It's yours."

"And I should believe you because . . . ?"

I sighed. "You shouldn't. I'm the last person

you should trust. I know that. But I swear I'm done with popularity." I reached down and flicked my Skin-covered forearm for emphasis. "I don't want this. And you do. You can have your old life back. And I'll have mine." I swallowed. "Please."

Slowly, as if moving in some sort of time warp, Kylie unfolded her arms. "Fine." She turned and headed silently up the stairs. I decided not to wait for an invitation and followed.

Kylie's bedroom was different now. The friendship collages were gone, as was the shot of her and Tanner. The only pictures in the room were a photo-booth strip of her and Ella and a large framed picture of a guy in a soccer uniform.

Matt Kane, I realized, staring at the image. The guy Kylie dumped for Tanner, way back when.

Kylie's eyes followed mine. "It's nothing serious," she said quickly. "We're sort of taking things slow."

I smiled at her. "I hope it works out."

She stared at me for a few seconds, then turned abruptly and cut across the room, stopping in front of her desk. Reaching into the first drawer, she pulled out a single piece of paper and held it out. "Here."

I glanced down at the plain white sheet,

trying to hide my disappointment. I guess I'd been expecting something a little fancier. Flowery gold script and heavy parchment that crackled when you turned the page, all bound in thick silk ribbons.

THE SECOND SKIN—RULES AND REGULATIONS

1. RESPECT THE SECOND SKIN AND IT WILL RESPECT YOU.
2. ONLY ONE SKIN IS PERMITTED PER SCHOOL.
3. DO NOT TELL ANYONE ABOUT THE SECOND SKIN.*
4. THE SECOND SKIN MUST NOT BE REMOVED FOR LONGER THAN FOUR HOURS AT ANY ONE TIME.

PLEASE SEE MANUAL FOR REMOVAL AND CARE GUIDELINES.

*(Since the Skin is invisible, you need not worry about embarrassing locker room scenarios. It is advised, however, that communal dressing rooms be avoided. Skin or no Skin, they're simply unpleasant.)

I read through the list once, then twice more. Each time, I could feel new lines popping up on my forehead.

Great, I thought. *Talk about vague. I'd get better directions from a fortune cookie.*

"Not too specific, is it?" I said aloud.

Kylie shrugged. "Well, I broke rule three and look what happened to me." She shot me a look. "You being a total jerk helped, of course."

Ignoring her, I stared down at the list. "But it doesn't tell me what I'm supposed to do."

Kylie groaned. "Not that this is in any way my problem, but in the interest of getting you out of my room as fast as possible, I'll give it a stab." She glanced over my shoulder, chewing on her lower lip as her eyes moved down the paper. "I don't know. Maybe you didn't respect the Skin? I mean, you did steal it." She leaned over and sniffed my arm, wrinkling her nose in distaste. "And you definitely didn't wash it enough. That thing's filthy. I really wish you'd swiped the care guide."

"Uh, thanks," I said, handing the paper back.

Kylie shrugged again. "Whatever."

"Look," I said. "I really am sorry."

Kylie turned away. "Why don't you go home and see if you can get it off? Then we'll talk," she said, her back stiff.

I hopped down the stairs and out onto the front porch. The Skin felt so tight I wondered if I even looked three-dimensional anymore. It was a geometry problem only Alex could solve.

Alex.

My heart twisted. How was I going to fix this?

The list of rules floated around inside my head, making me dizzy. *Respect the Skin . . . avoid communal dressing rooms . . .* true, I'd done none of those things. But I'd made so many other mistakes, too. It was hard to know where to start.

I guess sometimes you just have to wing it, I thought. I reached the edge of the porch, squeezed my eyes shut and jumped.

THIRTY-ONE

Since I'd never dumped anyone before (to be fair, I'd never had anyone to dump), I was a little nervous when I called Tanner the next morning to end things. Thankfully, he made it pretty easy.

"Wait, I don't get it," he said. He was holding the phone way too close to his mouth and his words came out all warped and breathy.

"I think we should break up," I repeated, resisting the urge to wipe off the receiver.

There was a pause on the other end of the line, followed by a few more obscene-phone-caller-type exhales (was he doing stomach crunches or something?) and then another "I don't get it."

I tried a different approach. "I just don't think we have a whole lot in common. You like sports and I like . . ."

I trailed off, wondering what exactly I did like. Thanks to the Skin, I'd learned a lot about what I didn't like and wasn't good at: partying, gossiping, any activity that involved a midriff-baring uniform. But what did I really enjoy? I jogged my memory, trying to remember which, if any, of the millions of responsibilities I'd juggled over the past few months *hadn't* made me want to impale myself on a baton.

Decorations.

The word triggered a slide show in my head, filled with Spring Fling constellations. I smiled at the memory of all that sketching, painting and glittering. It had been hard. But I'd enjoyed it. And I'd done a good job.

"Art," I finished. "I'm an—I'm sort of an artist."

"Well," Tanner said uncertainly. "That's cool. Maybe you could decorate my lacrosse jersey. Something different, you know? I could leave it for the school when I graduate."

Okay, third time's the charm. I gave it another shot. "There are a million girls out there who'd die to go out with you," I told him.

"That's true," Tanner said easily.

"I just think maybe you'd be happier with one of them," I pushed. "To be honest, I feel like I've been sort of monopolizing you." I paused and then tagged on a hasty, "I mean, holding you back."

"I can see that," Tanner said. "I guess I should get out there a little more—it's senior year."

"Exactly," I said, relieved to finally be getting through. "You should have fun. You owe it to yourself. And don't worry about me. I know we'll always be friends."

"Huh? Oh yeah, definitely." Tanner's voice was distant now and I had the feeling I'd caught him mid-hang-up. "Listen, I'll see you around, okay?"

And then he was gone.

I enjoyed the dial tone for several seconds, then hung up and left Jules a voice mail. I wasn't going to meet her—or any of the other pepsters—for a mani/pedi. I didn't care if it meant a lifetime of hangnails and calluses. I was through with all things A-list.

And, if my plan worked out, by the end of the day the A-list would be through with me, too.

I headed downstairs. My mother was in the living room slicing up the newspaper. She looked up. "You're home," she said, surprised.

"Uh, yeah," I said, shifting my weight from leg to leg. "I know I haven't been around so much lately."

My mother clicked her tongue and returned to her shredding.

"I just want you to know," I said, "that I'm sorry. I'm gonna cut back on all the school stuff—pep squad and everything." I watched as the scissors paused and, slowly, my mother raised her head from the newspaper. "I guess I was just trying out some different things but you were right all along. None of that stuff was really me."

"Oh, Sam," she said. "I'm so glad. I hope—"

"But listen," I said, rushing on. "I know you and Dad have really strong convictions. And I think that's great. But you can't just expect me to have them because I'm your kid. I don't think stuff like that's always . . . automatic."

My mother cast me a long, measuring glance. "I guess I hadn't really thought about it in those terms."

I shrugged. "I'm not saying I won't believe in the same things you do. You just need to let me figure it out for myself."

My mother placed her scissors on the table and reached for her coffee mug. "Well," she said. "I think you're off to a good start. That was a very mature speech, Sam."

I smiled. "Thanks."

"I might not seem like it," she said, after a long sip. "But I have—I've always had—a lot of faith in you. I know you'll make good choices." She paused. "Just try to stay away from a career in advertising, okay? I can handle anything but that."

I laughed. "I'll see what I can do. By the way, I'm borrowing the car." I grabbed the keys from the counter and headed out the front door.

Tanner. Jules. My mom.

Three down, two to go.

If the last two didn't kill me, this just might work.

THIRTY-TWO

"That'll be seventy-three dollars," announced the cashier.

I passed him my mother's credit card (it was for emergency purposes only, but this definitely qualified) and watched as he bagged the five CDs—all from top-ten artists—I'd just purchased. He handed me my receipt and I headed out to the parking lot. I popped one of the CDs into the car stereo and drove over to Gwen's house.

This has to work, I prayed as I shifted the car into park and lined the driveway with the remaining four CDs. I slid back behind the wheel, rolled down the windows and turned the music up. Way up.

And, just to make extra sure I wasn't ignored, I leaned on the horn.

"Are you crazy?" Gwen asked as she rushed out of her house. She was barefoot, wearing her apron over sweats.

"Sorry," I said, turning off the music. "I just wanted to get your attention."

"What are you even doing here? Shouldn't you be riding on top of a float?"

I shook my head. "Not anymore." I toyed with my key chain. "From now on, I'm float-free. I swear."

I took a deep breath, shifted the car into drive and slammed my foot on the gas. I could hear the CDs crunch under the tires as I flattened pop music.

I stopped the car at the bottom of the driveway and watched Gwen approach. Even from a distance I could tell she was fighting back a smile.

"Look," I started in as soon as she reached me. "I'm really sorry. About everything. I took you for granted. And I should've punched Chuck Todd for making that stupid comment at the dance."

"You're right," Gwen said, her voice bitter. "You did. And you should have."

I nodded. "I wish I could erase everything

that happened. But maybe it's good that I can't."
I shifted my eyes to the ground but could still
feel Gwen staring at me, trying to measure my
sincerity. "I think this whole thing sort of
helped me, I don't know, prioritize." I shifted my
weight from leg to leg, as much as the Ziplocked
Skin would allow. "It made me realize how lucky
I was. I just had no idea."

Gwen looked down at the smashed discs. "You
know," she said slowly. "I'm really glad you got
your brain back." When she raised her head, her
face was serious. "And I'm sorry too."

I stared at her. "What for?"

"I've been thinking about it a lot, and I guess
I can be a *little* judgmental," she said, frowning
slightly. "But I'm really trying—well, as of this
morning—to be more open-minded about meeting
new people . . . and school in general."

"Thanks," I said. "That means a lot."

Gwen shivered. "It's freezing out here," she
said. "Wanna come inside? I was making pancakes."

"Sounds great. I'm starving."

I slid my arm around her shoulder. Did the
Skin feel a little looser? It was hard to tell. And
at the moment, I didn't really care.

★ ★ ★

Stuffed with pancakes, my face green, I was standing in the middle of Alex's bedroom, watching him through the open window as he assembled his telescope on the roof of his porch.

I could see him but he couldn't see me.

I took a deep breath and walked toward him.

This probably won't work, I thought as I climbed through the window. *But at least I'll know I tried.*

"Hey," I said softly, appreciating the sun in Alex's black curls. His hair was so dark it took on a blue tint, even in the light.

Alex snapped the lens onto the end of the telescope. "Um, you do know that your face is bright green, don't you?" he said without looking up.

"I know. I wore it in honor of that day at the beach. My quarter birthday." I swallowed. "It—it was one of my favorite days."

Alex shrugged. "Great. I'm happy for you." He swung the telescope around, almost hitting me. "Listen, I'm a little busy here, okay? Good luck with the whole face-painting thing."

"I know I totally blew it," I blurted out. My voice sounded thick. "I know you hate me. *I* hate me." I sniffed. "But I came here to apologize . . . and to tell you that the reason the day at the beach is my favorite is because of you. *You're* my favorite."

Alex stood and turned to me. "What do you want me to say here, Sam?" he asked. "You lied to me. You took me to that dance and then left me standing there. I was finally trying to . . ." He cleared his throat and shoved his hands into his pockets. "You kissed that idiot like I didn't even exist."

"I'm so sorry," I repeated, staring down into the front yard. "But just so you know—that whole night, I was completely freaked out. Because of you." I bit my lip, then pushed on before I completely lost my nerve. "And the only reason I let Tanner kiss me was to see if it was possible to be in love with your best friend without even knowing it." I raised my eyes to meet Alex's. "It turns out it is possible. It happens."

Alex stared at me.

I placed the round container of zinc oxide at the base of the telescope. "You should have this," I said softly, turning back toward the window. "The sun is a lot stronger than you think."

I was halfway across the room when I heard the crash. As I turned toward the noise Alex grabbed me, looping his arms around my waist.

"I've thought about doing this for so long," he said. "But I never once pictured you with a green face."

I leaned into Alex's body and felt the Skin

give, ever so slightly. I smiled. And then Alex's lips met mine and I forgot . . . everything.

Much, much later—after we wiped the zinc oxide from our faces and picked pieces of telescope off the front lawn—I climbed back into the car and drove home. And when I stopped at a red light, I waved my hands high over my head and stretched. Just because I could.

THIRTY-THREE

"Here ya go," I said, thrusting the "I Am Not a Plastic Bag" bag toward Kylie. It was her old life.

And she was welcome to it. After returning home from Alex's house, I'd easily stripped off the Skin. No bends, twists or contortions. This time around, it slid from my body like a plus-sized girdle. I'd scooped it up and tossed it into the green felt bag without even a second of hesitation.

I was more than ready to say goodbye to popularity.

Standing in the middle of Kylie's bedroom, I

was certain that *this*—the original Samantha Klein—was my new-and-improved self.

Kylie smiled but kept her arms firmly planted by her sides. "Thanks," she said lightly. "But you know what? I'm good. I don't want it."

I gaped at her. "What are you talking about? Isn't this what . . . I mean, I thought you were so mad at me—"

"I was," Kylie said. "What you did was pretty awful."

I swallowed. "It was. I feel terrible."

"I know," Kylie said as she twisted the end of her ponytail around her fingers. "I've been thinking about it a lot, and the thing is, I sort of like my life without the Skin." She shrugged. "I have Ella, and things with Matt are going pretty well. Plus, I'm getting along with my parents for like the first time ever." She smiled. "I know it sounds pretty lame, but I guess I'm sort of liking me right now. I mean, at least I know this is me, right?"

"I can't believe I'm saying this, but I know exactly what you mean," I said. I looked at her. "Hey, did you ever wonder who sent it to you? Why *you* were chosen?"

Kylie bit her lip. "I don't know. Maybe a little. At first. Then I got so caught up with everything I just let it go."

"Well, maybe we could find out?" I suggested, my voice rising with excitement. "You know, hunt down the source?"

Kylie frowned. "And do what?"

"We could, I don't know, destroy it somehow," I went on, though I was starting to feel a little ridiculous. "And the Skin too. We could even locate the others and . . ." I trailed off as Kylie started to giggle.

"What, like a popularity quest?" she asked, smiling. "I don't know. That sounds sort of time-consuming. I've got a paper due Monday."

I laughed. "I guess it is a little ambitious."

"How about we just hide it for now?" Kylie suggested. "I don't think either of us is going to be tempted anymore, and this way no one else can use it either."

So we folded the Skin and put it in the back of Kylie's closet. As the door slid shut, I felt myself relax. Finally and completely.

"Well," Kylie said. "I guess that's that."

I nodded but made no move to leave. There was one last thought needling me, and I knew it was now or never.

"About last night," I said. "I just sort of lost it. I, uh, I know you weren't trying to steal my friends or anything."

"Yeah, that's what I was trying to tell you,"

Kylie said. "But you were too busy freaking out. Ella and I just ran into them when we were getting ice cream. We all decided to boycott the dance together." She leaned against the doorframe. "It was actually a lot of fun. Your friends are cool."

"Uh, well, maybe we could all hang out sometime. I promise not to throw another fit on your porch."

"Sounds good."

"So, I guess that's it," I said, turning to go.

Kylie cleared her throat. "Um, what are you doing now?" she asked hesitantly. " 'Cause I'm not busy and so I thought that maybe, you know, since we're neighbors . . ."

"Hey," I said, feeling hopeful. "Where do you stand on pop?"

Kylie raised her eyebrows. "Pop? Like soda?"

"No, you know, like the music," I clarified. "I mean, Gwen hates it, but . . ."

Kylie nodded. "Oh, Ella can't stand that stuff either."

There was a pause as Kylie and I eyed each other, considering.

"I've got this great CD in my car," I blurted out.

"I've got all Madonna's videos on my DVR," Kylie said quickly.

We laughed and, together, headed downstairs.

Caroline Wallace

While *Jessica Wollman* has never owned a magical suit of any kind, she's still hopeful that one might turn up. She has written numerous books for kids of all ages and lives in New York with her husband and a small menagerie of ill-mannered pets. You can visit her online at www.jessicawollman.com.